Come Send Thy Chariot

Ryan Dean Williams

In memory of Dr. Douglas "Doug" Mattox

~

Papa,

When the Chaplain came in you said:
This is my grandson, the writer.

I had not written anything yet, and you had not left us either.
But I shook her hand and something felt different.

Now all I have are words, and I don't know if that makes me a writer.
Maybe it was when you called me one.

yours,

Ryan

She put her hand to the nail, and her right hand to the workmen's hammer; and with the hammer she smote Sisera, she smote off his head, when she had pierced and stricken through his temples.

~

The mother of Sisera looked out at a window, and cried through the lattice,
Why is his chariot so long in coming? Why tarry the wheels of his chariots?

Judges 5:26, 28 KJV

April 23, 1971

Brier. Thorned, shields itself from danger, and unthorned is vulnerable to the world. Winter comes. The frozen, spindly branches cannot defend from predators. The true weapon has been made futile. The Brier, with its thorns, creates safety for itself by appearing dangerous to others. Without this danger, the protection leaves also.

The long winter wanes and the Brier moves its arms. The ground thaws. The sharp edges are unsheathed and dangerous again, and therefore the Brier is safe. When the fruit comes, it will be protected. But can the seed sustain— will its family grow? There is a change; the air is thick with pollen. Nature leans on its toes. Spring is ready to break.

Dean Elliot

When I called my father to tell him I passed the bar, he told me death made good business.

"There's another Elliot in law now. How about it, old man?"

"Great, Dean—look into wills. There's money there."

"You bet, Pop."

"Remember Paul though," he said. "Smart kid. Smart enough to know the right path."

My father had to do it—bring up Paul, someone from law school he liked. It was always the old ghosts. At the worst times and in the worst ways. Just when I had made a name for myself, another name had to cast itself across the embers of my ambition, extinguishing the glory.

Unlike then, my father had always left a lot unsaid. That's how I remembered him when I became the only Elliot in law—God rest his soul. But he was right about death for one thing, and I thought again about what my father told me when I visited a client of mine by the name of Laithe.

Old man Laithe went by 'The Captain' to everyone in town; including me, despite having more information about him than all of Newburg did (courtesy of attorney-client relationship). The commonfolk had been calling him this ever since he told them there was nothing—not even

Captain Laithe—that he would answer to other than The Captain, so it made my work easier to follow the crowd.

I had my doubts when I first visited him at his residence—taking a few wide glances around that estate on the hill, walking up the long drive that slanted into the sky with forests of scarred timber encircling the lot—to see the juxtaposition of his manhood harshness: the bloodroot blossoms edging his garden and growing along the path that led to the back of the house. The Captain even had a book of Missouri wildflowers that he would flip through, pausing on the page of a certain kind to share its significance to him. He insisted he could trace back most of his lineage to that land.

Both great and lousy men had put their mark on it one way or another. The stone-walled and glassy-eyed façade, with its menacing physique, dug its heels into the footings by leaning forward with the support of strong timbers buffeting the foundation from the rear. It was a sturdy wood—mahogany strength with southern pine ancestry—and since the estate was the largest asset to the Laithe name, it was the only matter he agreed to discuss with me when his health began to decline.

The Captain wanted to know how to give the estate to his eldest son, Philmore, after his own uncle passed; and if Philmore died early also, he insisted it pass "right on down the line" to all the Laithes you could hit with a stone's throw from the porch. Indeed, it seemed plausible from the top of the hill, looking down the dew-touched drive that dropped into the river valley below and surveying the township of Newburg where his few living relatives remained. I didn't realize how serious The Captain had been until after he passed. It was then that I truly became acquainted with the estate and its constituents.

Fanny Brier was the only mother of any of The Captain's children whose whereabouts were really known. She took up a permanent place at the estate as the fill-in for a housewife and a deputy of matronly affairs. Fanny herself was already getting on in years, but even so, she kept the children fed and clothed while maintaining a standard of cleanliness unbeknownst to most households with three youth-frustrated and fatherless pupils. In her care, the boys became a kind of pride before they knew it, and soon they reached an age where they could even be called grown and still narrowly escape this realization themselves.

Philmore was away from the house most of the day and did not return until the sun was down. He worked in the mines north of Newburg, in the crescent-shaped cleft of Phelps County where trains carrying freight came barreling through the country from the coasts. Philmore's job demanded much of him. He was up at first light and toiled under the soil and under the graves of the great and lousy men who were his forefathers, working for the right to keep the estate. Philmore took care of his younger brother—the middle child, Benton—who didn't trade his years but rather gave them up to the military, fighting its wars and becoming haunted by the ghosts of his father's regalia and military honor. For the holy grail and mantel of the Laithes's pride was to behold The Captain's war, which had been real and winnable. But this was not the same appraisal given to Benton's war. Society had labeled it a skirmish waged on the 17th parallel, a non-war splitting two non-countries and fought over whose blood was non-blood and whose was chosen blood—a tale as old as the Israelites and the sons of Abraham and Isaac and Jacob.

Benton returned from his non-war with a concoction of discovered trauma and preexisting cognitive disabilities that were already widely known and genetic—a penance for the sins of his father. His mental illness had tapered off enough for him to learn to hold a rifle and shoot it true, and enough for most of the world to forget about his condition, forcing king and country to draft him without a second glance at his medical history. And the effects weren't much deeper than the surface. Benton's bouts came in frequent and unpredictable surges that only the youngest brother, Jedediah, had a real knack for handling with dignity and care. In fact, Benton received more attention from Jedediah than his own mother, Fanny Brier, who was too preoccupied with tidiness and correctness or having dignity of her own to worry about her son; as it was her relations with the late Captain that had ruffled the feathers of the town.

Fanny and her cousin, some say, were the spittle that ran down from the mouth of central Missouri. If a proper marriage constituted honor and a clean name, the Laithes found only shame and a battered reputation from the acts of the two who had always lived within a mile from each other. Benton was the fruit of their sin, and both The Captain and Fanny knew it. Right after Benton's limitations were diagnosed in his unknowing infancy, both of them came running to the church to baptize the child and 'get the devil out.' That's when Reverend Milton bid the family return to the altar for their own sanctification. Miraculously, they did.

Fanny had been living with her husband, who was not the father of Benton but pretended to be; that is, until Mr. Brier found out that he wasn't and left one evening without saying goodbye—leaving his house to be foreclosed and Fanny to move in with her father, Allan Laithe, and the very cousin she had committed her incestuous affair with. But I will give her credit. Even a year later, when The Captain's failing heart killed him, Fanny took care of things better than I expected given the nature of an estate void of honor and a name unfit for pride.

It wasn't until Fanny's death that I really believed what my own father had told me all those years ago when I finished law school. But I didn't attend her funeral for business. I went for reassurance that the Laithes would not die out as I feared. My practice was beginning to be questioned in light of the rumors surrounding the family's scandal and my deciding to represent them. Some even accused Philmore and Jedediah of also being inbred, but those two didn't have the mental disorders to back an allegation of too many common genes.

Reverend Milton did not agree with me on the graveness of the future of the Laithes until recently. I described to him my first visit to that robust but brittle estate—a ground on which aspirations of boyhood met the fever dream of Missouri manhood—where men worked the long hours of the day away and the tidiness of the home fell on the shoulders of the women. In the case of Fanny Brier, whatever order she had brought to the estate was vanquished in her passing. It therefore took Reverend Milton no time at all to concur that honor had become stagnant, that greatness had curdled with her death, or, paramount: that there were still three sons of a man half-great and half-despised who together could be the redemption for their shared name.

The three—Jedediah, Benton, and Philmore—made the half-blood pact of one dead father and three unknown mothers (except for Benton's, of course) whose ghosts lived in the shadows of the Gothic stone house standing on a sort of hallowed ground. That enduring image moved me so: the stonework appearing monolithic in the afterglow of the dying day and Philmore returning from the mines to a house with no woman to keep it. It was harrowing, as if I had looked for the remains of his buried kin in the hillside, or the faces of his dead ancestors in the streams, but found instead the silhouettes of him and his brothers against the sun-warmed water—their boyhood figures reflected in the very trout pools where The Captain had taught them each the discipline of the catch.

I told Reverend Milton I would talk to Philmore after Fanny's memorial, but he didn't seem as worried as I was. We came at it from different sides.

"There is faith and there is reason, Reverend." I told him. "What if they won't hear either?"

"There's not a dozen. My, there might not even be half a dozen men this side of the grave that could see their boyhood home go rotten." Reverend Milton said. "I say, let God be the judge of The Captain and Fanny's sins, seeing that now they are both united on the other side of death." He paused here before finishing his thought. "Let Philmore either take the helm or go down with the ship."

This idea of dissociating with the family had given me peace of mind for one whole day. I told the reverend again after the memorial that I could not let it rest, and that I would talk with Philmore after his trip to Jefferson City. I told Milton of Philmore's intentions with a certain solemnity, recollecting the haste with which Phil excused himself from me after Fanny's service and said he would have to miss her burial to see about a coal delivery. *Did a man's work not take a break in such a time as this?*

That day I took the proverbial helm myself, accepting that it must be me who would brace the town for the Laithe family's fall; and all the while, unaware that it had already begun. Yet my ultimate conviction, even if it proved to be a dishonorable attempt at using my office and my education in reaching outside of the confines of law, was to become the orator and recorder of the Laithes's affairs. I intended not to memorialize the slow deterioration of their legacy, but, more hopefully, to prevent it. It was my mission to divulge the truth, seeking information through more than just the statutes of my discipline. Nevertheless, my single great concern in thus exposing the secrets of such a family was the forfeiture of my practice as an attorney by executing the duties of a journalist.

After remembering my reasons for making the decision, I knew I must continue. For it had been my conviction to strive for truth which had pushed me to study law, and that also which would require me to abandon it. I saw clearly enough now to reveal my motivator: I felt troubled for the heirs of my late client. Therefore, if I did nothing of more merit, I intended to publish an unbiased account of my personal dealings with the family. I would appeal to the ears of those who wished to know things as they were and not as they were made out to be. Despite years of incomplete truths and false rumors circulating among the people of Newburg, I hoped to salvage a fraction of honor for the heirs of the Laithe family estate and bring peace to the restless spirits of their forefathers. It was the undying dignity of those tortured souls that I could feel stirring at the mention of the Second Death, which awaited a man when his name was tarnished.

Philmore

A man can't know a piece of lan' till he's gone under it. And no one who's ain't been under the surface of the earth could ever know't that a'way. That's the difference 'tween the man that tills the ground and the man that mines it. Jed knows the soil and the lan' just about good as anyone can by standin' on its face, but not near good as those who work in its belly. See, he works the field and brings in the crop, curses the ground when it's bad and praises it when it's easy on him. But there's no natural goodness in the earth that I seen—it either damns or chooses not to.

The mines in the caves under the lan' lie in a throat of darkness, and there ain't any light until you tunnel far enough or long enough to find it. Some say there is. But I never seen it. I don't crack the rock open to find the light. I do it for the money. I got a family to keep alive and that ain't easy with them dyin' off one and two and three. But I reckon ol' Fanny knows the lan' better than any of us now that she's gone under it.

Her casket was the workmanship of fine hands toiling just like she'd done in that estate all them years, but boxed up into just a coupl'a days. Now I figured it was almost my estate. Fanny was the last heir o' that line standing 'tween us and Uncle Allan, and with Fanny gone, he would pass the birthright on to me when he died. Then ol' Ben, and finally Jed. But Benton's the only one had the right to claim

Fanny as his mama, seeing he was the only one o' us who shared that last name. I tell you, it's an odd thing when you got a brother through and through but you don't have a common name—gets folks to ask'n questions.

Benton was called a Brier so's not to remind us all o' what our pops done. He told Fanny to give Benton her last name instead of his'n, so's to hide it from her husband who stayed too busy to know what was right under his nose. To old Mr. Brier, Benton was his'n. But soon he learnt the truth. All the while, Benton was truly a brother to me, same way as Jed, though Jed and I probably didn't have the same mom neither. See, probably our moms were two-bit whores that never saw past their youth, or at least not past our pops's wanderin' hands when he came home from the sea and told the town to call him The Cap'n. There was always plenty o' business in Newburg for girls who got to scamperin' about at night, and without much of a badge of shame neither—but even so, it's liken' to a sin around here to sleep with your kin no matter what. We lived in a small town but not a solitary one. So when Benton was born dumb, people got to ask'n.

"Say, Phil…" they'd a start, "you'se got the hair o' your daddy, but not the hair o' your mama."

"I'm singly shocked you seen it," I tells 'em. "Seeings I don't know my mama and never met her, and my daddy never knowed what came o' her 'fore he died—I'm singly shocked you seen what hair my mama had."

"But the whole lot o' you was raised by that Fanny, boy. How—"

"You right on the nail there, I reckon." I says, without lettin' them get on with it. "She felt like a mama 'cause she raised me, but she was only one true to Benton. Look at the name, there. It's a difference of Brier to Laithe." I tells 'em "Now, if you'll let me get on," I says, "I see that sun dying and every hour you keep ask'n me about is an hour I could be splittin' rock and making that name o' mine count."

Those folks lost their obsession with the scandal eventually, and I figured no one would bother me 'bout it now that Fanny found the light. But it really was a fine funeral. Her casket had a shine to it like the sweat of a laborer.

I stood there takin' it in, thinking on her memory, and who else came up to me, after the memorial, when the old folks were ask'n me about Fanny and sayin' their sorrys—who else than that lawyer of our'n, Dean Elliot?

"This is the hardest part," he said, or somethin' like it at least. "I know you'se trying to feel it all, but when you and them brothers a'yourn are ready, we needs to talk about keeping that estate."

I wasn't listenin' to him all that much with all the other stuff in my head. I kept thinkin' how Fanny knew the lan' more than any of us—more than me. *What was it made me think on death so much?* I knew what. It was folks like

16

that girl I met the week 'fore this'n, when I was on my way to the rock. Stopped me and asked if she could ask a couple things for some book she was writing. I didn't let her get very far.

"What's it about?" I says.

She said it was about the town.

"*Us?*" I says. "Listen good 'cause I'll only say it once: unless you're from this county, or at least from this state, you shouldn't be writing of it. You got that look of the sea in that hair of yourn—bet you'se from California or Oregon. Look, don't write about a ground your feet ain't been raised up on."

She looked a little scared and I knew I had her. These types were easy to spook. I knew if I played it right she'd never bother me again. I spat on the ground and asked where she was from. She looked shot. Didn't say nothin'.

"That's what I thought," I says. "Take that soft look in your eyes back where you came from."

I was already walking out of earshot when she gave me somethin' to think on.

"Westphalia," she says shaky as a colt. "I'm from Westphalia. Or Jefferson City—whichever you like."

"Born and raised," she went on, "but you ain't wrong about the sea in my hair. I had to get away. See the coast." She squared up her shoulders and lifted her head. "Now, look, I understand—get on to that rock; it's gonna be a scorcher today and I have others to talk to. Goodbye now."

I stopped in my tracks at that voice, and I knew I'd be coming back to it again 'fore I knew it. Maybe I was wrong about her. She could be a true Miss'ura woman. Westphalia was a town I knew. I'd passed through it drivin' up 63 plenty o' times—it was a harsh town, but somewhere I could plant a seed o' thought on and sew it 'cause I'd seen it before.

"I know Westphalia," I says to the back of her. "The one with the village on a hill, and the big steeple comin' straight out o' the ground from the crest o' the town. That's how I seen her."

She didn't say nothing, so I kept on. "What's your name, girl?"

She stopped. "Jacqueline," she says. Didn't even turn.

"Right then, Jackie. I'm Phil."

"Pleasure, Phil."

I felt rotten that she got me so easy after I had her first—that's how the fight went sometimes. The title holder'd come out strong but lose too many points on the counters. I was beat, I guess. I figured I'd let her wear the belt now. See how she handled it.

"Say, when I'm bringin' up a truckload to Jeff City, I'll stop by and answer them questions you'se ripe to ask," I says. "But I gotta get to that rock now." And I didn't think about her again till right after Fanny died a few days later.

Dean didn't waste a whole lotta time comin' to our property and tiptoein' around the estate after the funeral neither. My pops had been his client, then pops's Uncle Allan next (our Great Uncle then, I reckon, but we just called him Uncle Allan), so Dean had a bone to pick with me. I was next in line after Fanny found the light and wouldn't get the birthright. He told me what I already knew: that it would be my rightful lan' soon as Uncle Allan kicked it. I didn't give it much thought. To be honest, I figured Dean had his eyes set on all the money he could reap from the family payin' him to handle the inheritance. Made me sick, I'll say it—all that lawyer aimed to do was take and eat off another's plate.

Then sure enough I got to thinkin' about that little girl from Westphalia all over again. She was too young and too educated and too stupid and too pretty—the way I saw it those types were only ever trouble—but here I was, keeping the conversation short with ol' Dean boy and gettin' him to shut up about the lan' so I could go see her again.

"I gotta see about a girl, Mr. Elliot," I says. "Thank ya."

Guess I knew every moment I spent there thinkin' about a woman was a moment I could be with her—with a nice girl who would sit down with me in that house and take care o' things one day. Jackie wasn't just any ol' girl neither; no, not just any. She was the kind who got her brain from books. Smart as a whip, but she had a lot of unlearnin' to do too. I figured I'd make that trip up to Jeff City.

Jacqueline

'Jackie.' He called me 'Jackie.' It should've been nothing more than an accident, the butting of two animals that never see the other again; but there his voice was, clear, soft, iambic—it subdued me when rough men like him spoke in a simple way. *And he was right about California*, I thought driving up Route 63 later that day in the waning afternoon light. The West had been a lifetime ago; a young and stupid Midwest girl running away to where the Pacific Ocean spilled into Monterey to become a writer. Now, I was finally back where I was meant to be: Missouri—where I had missed the seasons and could see stories in the eyes of the men, the hard men, pushing coal carts in and out of the mines with dusty hands and blackened fingers. Steadily I rode further away from this Ozark land, away from the rough, handsome men, and closer to the place of my youth. Westphalia looked like a tiny patch sewn on a hill rising up from the river basin; it was the cloth that underpinned Jefferson City, the fabric that was discarded and made into a quilt of reusables which had no use itself.

It was clumsy of me to believe, but I did believe, that my strange encounter with the man from that morning was the beginning of the rest of my life—*and why not*? He was my Phil; or rather he must have become that, for I didn't believe time could mean one thing when you met someone your soul belonged to. He spoke to me, saying "Jackie, I'll stop by and answer these questions of yours." And he could not have known what questions he had meant—the kind of questions where you skipped right past the never-having-known and landed at the belonging-to another.

How did this man speak to my heart, reach his breath into my lungs, and pull out my thoughts, my dreams, and all my aspirations? He had almost walked away from me forever. My life was that close, that much of a moment, from being unlivable should he not have turned back at the mention of my hometown. This paranoia must have been the first symptom of my terminal condition—the inoperable illness of love that gripped my heart. But even still, I leaned into the disease with that unutterable four-lettered friend of it, hope, and believed that when Phil saw me again he would love me so.

It was new, or at least the feeling of being new. I was pleasantly caught up in a life only partially lived with the fresh sun on my skin and a warm breeze blowing up the street as I crossed it. I walked into my father's store and asked the young boy at the counter to fetch him. As I waited, I allowed the four-letter words to trickle in, to wreak havoc on me again. If Phil would just make me his, I would never have to stare at the blank pages next to my typewriter, at the myriad of unwritten manuscripts and dozens of envelopes enclosing the letters addressed to me, saying: "Not yet, but your writing is close. Needs more command of the language. Stay in touch."

San Francisco was too big a place for my writing to ever find significance. I moved and got a grant to write under a sponsor for a program in the Bay area whose agency would fund my first few attempts, giving me ample opportunity to pursue my dreams and arrive at that elusive and painstaking command of the language. My first love had removed all creative blocks, but when he left, so my passion did also. I learned there was a danger in writing for others; yet here it was, this feeling, this curiosity, for a Missouri man in the mines underground. And now in light of this Phil, my first love didn't haunt me anymore. My unwritten stories were no longer desolate canyons that could never be traversed. I arrived, truly, at genuine happiness—and what's more—at a sustainable outlet to write for the rest of my life. Through these romances, art could be made into a dirty but altogether dignified reflection of life. Perhaps he didn't love me as I had begun to love him; yet I decided, even so, that it would help me write the pain away all the same—that at last I could sit at my typewriter and write something true. So, in that way, I could only gain from him. I had defeated my own lust for love without ever achieving the object of it.

My thoughts were appending onto one another, multiplying and illuminating the next like the wicks of many candles tied together. I measured my motives again to be sure about my self-sustained victory, but before I could, a small boy came back to the counter and told me that my father was not there; "Must'a gone home early." A knot pressed against the walls of my stomach at once—for I knew he never left his shop, from open to close, unless something truly bad had happened.

That evening I pulled into our circle drive, killed the engine, and found my father lying on his back in the foyer. He was wrestling with a ghost it seemed. Rapid movements seized him. It did not look like my father at all but a terrifying projection of him. His eyes rolled back into his head, the feet curled inward on themselves at the toes, and his arms were bowed in a mechanical arc. I fell to the floor at the sight and felt a terror grip my heart as the air rushed out of my lungs. Looking at the phone, the turn-dial made no sense to me in this state, and the flecks and fading spots in front of my eyes turned my fear to a blind but embittered hysteria. I yelled to no one for anyone, and I suppose it was our neighbor that answered the call—telling me much later how he had been tending to his hydrangeas when he heard me yell: "Help, please help! He's having a stroke—someone, please!"

I went away from the Phil-hope in my head, but when I came back to it, I yearned for someone to lean on other than myself. I wanted a break from the horror of a life of unknown, or maybe just life itself, and how it had to nearly kill another for me to appreciate my own. My father was finally stable when the paramedics hoisted him onto the stretcher and carried him outside, crossing the flower beds he had always tended to. They treaded their feet clumsily, taking care not to drop him, and left the disrupted soil in their wake.

Benton

Fanny was dead.

There were circles in the sky; I saw big ones, small ones coming down. Rain. I smelled the drops in the air and smelled 'em hit the ground; mommy would never come up out the ground. There was a room with a chair where we rocked until I was older. And then she was gone but the room stayed. That day I woke up and saw the peelin' wallpaper with flowers on it. In the room with the rocking chair and thought of mommy when I ran my fingers over the frayed edges of the—Philmore. *Where's Philmore?* That's right. *Philmore's coming back tomorrow.*

There were big round circles coming down from the sky and my face was wet from the rain. I heard the reverend saying something about Fanny. She was dead. Fanny was my mother. I slept with her in the bed with one leg over her so she would never leave me in the dark room. They made a hole for her in the ground and I watched it swallow her and the casket in one go. We were together—me and Jedediah— in the graveyard. *Was Jed with me in the war?* No, I couldn't remember. If he was, I would'a remembered it. Yes.

I went away to war and mommy left also but in the other way. The reverend's voice came up into the air and spread out and fell down and we were together, Jedediah and me; *Jedediah was not in the army with me.* Now I had that straight. In war there was no end to the yellin' and shootin' and I had thought of home a lot and of the peelin' wallpaper until my head kept spinnin' all the long night long. I was a good kid, a normal kid. I never hurt nobody. But mommy's dead now so what did it count for? Yes, what did it count for. Daddy's funeral was better because there were less people and it was quieter.

All I heard was the reverend speakin' under the bullets in the sky coming down and I thought they were angels but I knew angels didn't shoot guns. Angels and God and heaven opened up gunfire onto the square plot of land and God was a chopper and a chopper was God when you had nothing but yourself and a M16 and a small ammo pack on your side. Two Hueys were in the air and about to touch down south of us. We were almost home. It was just a matter of exfil and rollin' out.

"It's Christ's second coming," said the Major, when he saw one of the helicopters settin' its feet down in the clearing. Then he answered a call from base and I thought I saw him about to cry. He was jittery and clutching the short-distance radio when he heard the call come in from Lieutenant Marsh loud over the intercom.

"We're aborting the mission. Lost a chopper. Have to evacua—" The signal went out. And the Major wept for the first time in the war.

So that's how I found out Christ wasn't comin' a second time like the Scriptures said. *But maybe Phil would come back.* It was like I was there again—I could even hear the rifles. Crack of 21 rifles and then quiet. I saw myself in the war and Fanny was there too but dead in a foxhole. Her grave made me snap back from the shock of the guns and soon as I know it I'm shakin' in Jedediah's arms. It was springtime in Miss'ura when the Bradford pear trees bloomed along the slopes of the grassy hills where Jedediah held me—I didn't know if Philmore would ever come back. *Reckon was I even back yet?* Two Hueys; two clicks from the LZ—blades beatin' the air.

The funeral was like the war and Jedediah and I came back to the house up a long drive up the hill, as brothers, like when you just went through the same thing together. Anyone else goes through it and you reckon they're your brother too. Philmore must've been killed too. He wasn't in the war though. Only seeing about a girl. *What was the difference?*

He didn't even wait till after the burial to leave. There was no honor anymore but now there were two Bentons. The one from before Vietnam and the one after. One made it home at least. I thought of mommy's funeral again. The smell of the wet cemetery with sunshine after a rain. With clouds movin' away and Benton better again. The people from the other burial had left and Reverend Milton had gone away and it was like war did too. It was almost all right except that Phil was gone, but I knew he would be back the next day.

Jedediah

Not one bitch in the whole litter. That was all I could think of at the time, 'cause Benton looked just like my hound givin' birth earlier that morning.

"Shh, shh, it's alright," I said to Ben. "It's alright." And I thought of my .357 while I was holding him.

My eyes saw the hound dog again from the morning all bloated with its belly out and just havin' pushed the last life out of her body, and the four puppies sucking her tits and not one o' them a bitch. I would need to buy a new one. I looked at Ben again and it made me sick. I wished he was only a dog and it was as easy as it was that morning when I brought her over by the creek, just under a nook of shade where the water ran nice and smooth, and let her go of the pain. The barrel was hot and smoking afterwards. I set the muzzle on the ground while I pushed the bitch into the creek and let her body float down. I gathered the four hound pups and took 'em back to the Kubota.

Benton was no hound, but it was hard to see the human in him right then when he got to shakin' and cryin'. It was just him and me and the reverend, and then even the reverend left. I shushed him in his ear and patted him on the chest. I thought of the hound one more time and listened to the cicadas hush out the whole rest of the world. The military burial on the other side of the cemetery finished up and the folks were gettin' in their cars. The cicadas rattled loud on account the rain had just died and the sun was finally out. Ben's chest was heavin' big still, but least ways he was done jerking in my arms for a little while, so I stopped thinkin' about the bitch. I *was* gonna have to get another one though.

People and animals were all the same at the end of their time, 'cause they were only ever good for keeping their name going and planting their seed. Philmore was doin' just that right about then, though I wasn't so sure about it until he'd told us after the memorial that he was goin' out o' town and wouldn't make it to the burial. I knew it was about a girl, but he never even told me her name—just that she was from Westphalia. Anyway, I reckoned that when the oldest brother left, and the middle brother was like a dying hound that you couldn't put down, it made the youngest 'take the helm'— just like Dean always told us. I got to thinkin' 'bout the house all o' sudden, and where Fanny's dyin' left us, and it didn't feel no good to man the ship when it was in that state. I hoped Phil would come back all right, not all delusional with the strange, near-death itch of startin' a family like a hound gets when he knows his time is coming soon. Though, if he did come back with a woman I wouldn't need to look after Ben so much.

Benton never had a choice when the nation went to war, and we weren't good enough of a nation to stop him from goin' anyway. From birth, he'd always had some loose screws 'cause o' what happened 'tween Fanny and The Cap'n, and 'Nam only made it worse. Go figure. You take a dog that lost its kick already, put it under some strain and stress, shoot at it a few times with fully automatic rifles while it's layin' in a ditch with nothin' around it but other dead; and after that, you throw some grenades at it and say it can't go on leave until it does two more missions; you do all that, and more than likely that dog won't be able to tree a coon or do anything useful when it comes back home. And that's about what all hounds are good for when they didn't start out well and got used even worse.

I picked Benton up from the dirt 'cause we had to get a move on, but I must'a started too quick for him. Had to be extra sensitive with that ol' boy. Finally we did get out o' the cemetery. As we left, I saw a nice, shady spot by some trees with a small creek running through, and before I knew it I was thinkin' how I needed a new bitch again.

Reverend Milton

I cleared my throat and heard a murmuring in the crowd, a shuffling of anxious hands and feet. Whether it was there or not, I couldn't have known. I simply heard it or pretended to so I could speak with conviction.

"Today we consecrate Fanny Brier. Trusting you, Lord God, our Father, to give her spirit safekeeping. Asking your Son, who shed His most precious blood on Calvary for Fanny and the rest of us sinners, to interpose once again with the blood of the Lamb, rescue her soul, and bring her to your glory. In submitting to the Holy Spirit—*Yes, God. We submit to you*—who moves within us and makes straight the path to holiness, we strive toward the hope of your Promise. Be with those who are mourning, Father God, and draw near to the brokenhearted as it says in your Word. Make us your children again, though we disobey, and answer our prayer to heal those who grieve. I offer Fanny's only son, Benton, to you this day. He is one of these grieving hearts, Lord. I pray that there would be a renewal of life despite the bereavement of—"

The 21-gun salute sounded out nearby at this time, and that was a travesty for two reasons. It was a small cemetery, and there was not much room to spread out before being almost at the boundary—a hedgerow and creek which could only be crossed on a small footbridge—and the more important reason: the presence of the war-torn Benton Brier.

It was a miracle he was even there, in attendance of his own mother's funeral. He had received official leave after his whole company was ambushed in the night, a night which he endured only by playing dead in his foxhole.

Back at base his C.O. gave him medical leave, and Benton got word shortly after his plane landed in St. Louis that his mother had also been ambushed in the night, only this was an ambush by her failing constitution rather than the Vietcong. Whether his reaction to the 21-gun salute was a way of playing dead again—his only learned measure of survival—or an expression of his genuine shock at the death of his mother, can only be guessed. I simply recall that one moment he stood there, privately turning his grief over in his hands, and the next he was shaking in Jedediah's arms from the shock that each consecutive report of the rifles created within his spirit. It was a shame that there had to be another burial in the same small lot, on the same day, and in such a loud fashion. I prayed that Jedediah, who sat there with his eyes glazed over, muttering hatred under his breath, wouldn't lash out at the men across the cemetery who had only fired in reverence. For though there was honor in the death of a soldier, to Benton it was as if there had been no pride in his own war, no veneration like there had been in the war of his father, or of this faceless soul on the other side of the cemetery. To those without the trauma of war, the ceremony on display was sweet as bird calls, and it rang and died out peacefully over the hills in solemn remembrance.

The clouds were hanging low now, and I saw the youngest—though himself not a son of Fanny—holding Benton and whistling his brother a quiet tune to relax his body. It seemed to work, for though the eldest wasn't there to take care of his younger brothers and see that they mourn in their own ways, Jedediah acted as Philmore that day, caring for the man-child who was scarred by the horrors of combat. Nevertheless, I could not continue with the service after my blessing of the grave was cut short by the shots ringing out in the air and Benton reacting in such a frenzy of emotion; so I called all the family to place a hand on the casket before it was lowered down. Even Mr. Brier, Benton's fraudulent father, looked shaken, bereaved of his wife whom he had built the courage to separate from but never quite divorce after the scandal.

It was a sobering day but not a sad one. That is, there was a different feeling of heaviness: the kind that starts to tingle the muscles so that one knows the heart is still beating true. That day I knew I had not grown numb to death, for I took in the sight of Jedediah Laithe holding Benton Brier over a field of crude stones and stored it away. I looked out at the ridge of pear trees hanging over the western fence, and saw, just before lifting my face to the horizon, the headstone that marked the eternal rest of The Captain. I hoped in prayer that he had also taken in what I had between Jed and Ben, and that he would know his family would not be lost forever in the shadow of his grave.

I wondered where his soul perched. In the Scriptures, it holds that the thief must have been saved when he confessed that the martyr beside him on the cross was the Son of Man, and that Jesus meant what he said when he promised him they would be together that day in Paradise. On this side of death, it was never too late to offer your soul—I knew that from the story. Yet I couldn't make sense, my theological training notwithstanding, of a world where a man lived a life like The Captain's and was still forgiven in the end.

I left unremarkably from the cemetery. The wind rose, and the sun, which could finally be seen from behind the clouds, dipped down toward the western wall of slate-gray sky. The day was colder than it should have been. I asked Jedediah if he wanted me to wait for him to take Benton back to the estate on the hill, but he declined with a wordless sound. I thought about that house as I left the two brothers there, with its stone and woodwork and windows; that estate where the rest of their lives would play out, hidden from the sins of their father in the clefts of hill country.

August 17, 1979

    Barren. The sustenance of pre-death. A differentiable marker by which we can discern living, and unliving; yielding, and unyielding. For where can there be renewal without the barrenness preceding it? In a scorched land—not a dead land, there is a difference—it teaches the living where it comes from, then reveals the dust it must return to. There are no months in a barren place. No seasons by which time hangs its fruit. The vintage is the last of its line in the barren vineyard of age.

    The winemakers spoke about it before the time came. The inventory and how it would be sold off. "300 boxes left and your name on one if you want it. $60 bottles now at an hour wage." But there were no takers. They did not want fruit from a bad harvest, for they knew the grapes were not the finest. The finest had been picked long ago when land was living. When pre-death was actually a successor and not a predecessor. When fortune-tellers spoke backwards to warn the people of the barrenness in the land. And to tell them that even now, before the wine ran out, they were drinking the last vintage.

Dean Elliot

"Ladies and gentlemen of the great state of Missouri, there comes a time in human proceedings when a man must stand before the people he once represented; who seek to spit in the face of his civil duty; who question or possibly even denounce his honorable name in the courts; and who plead for reasoning from him: a man so estranged that he would offer counsel in this civil case and bring to completion that which has only recently been undone. Today marks nearly 15 years since I took an oath to defend and intercede for the good people of Phelps County, and it is true that I have represented the Laithe family of Newburg township for over half my time as probate attorney. It is also true that my tenure will have concluded at the completion of this address, as I am making an official announcement of my retirement from law and the closing of my practice.

"During various proceedings of society in which I have been in the public eye, serving in its trials and taking up the defense of its people, I have not sought to gain from those whom I have represented. Nor did I put myself in a position to take from my clients, despite the accusations that I have been only interested in the money wrapped up in the Laithe estate. Rather, in my time in the Phelps County courts, I have been watching that same society with shrewdness—developing a keen understanding of the citizens of Newburg. I have seen this day approaching for eight summers now, and nearly eight autumns, after the death of Fanny Brier brought me to know and accept the limitations of my office—a day which must come to fruition now in the era of relative peace following the settling of the family's inheritance. It has greatly exhausted my faculties to represent the family for the last two years, beginning with Philmore Laithe's death and only just having drawn to a close with his widow's recent remarriage. Even so, as I merge with that society and integrate with its citizenry, it is merely the end of one calling and the start of another. Under the eyes of state and country, I will devote myself to a different but equally pressing cause, taking up my pen and paper in service of that greater war— the war waged in the frontiers of public opinion—and seek the truth without hiding behind the veil of law.

"In closing, I believe that I have exercised my duty in office faithfully, and leave the stand today with sincere pride in the work I have accomplished. I demanded a fervor of myself that breached upon the firmament of mental sanity, and pushed it even beyond this. I therefore owe it to myself and my fellow Statesmen to withdraw with my remaining convictions intact. Indeed, as many of you have surely heard, I aim to cover the story of the Laithes—not from the perspective of a circumstantial witness, nor from the guileless window of a judge's eye, but as an impartial and motivated journalist for the remaining heirs of the family— whose property remains the pride of the hills of Newburg.

"Following the two-year anniversary of the death of Philmore Laithe, I am tempted with idleness but defy it with the magnanimous call to action from my first client, the late Roger "The Captain" Laithe. He told me many years ago, that 'in all the land, there were three things to remember— Brier, Barren, and Bloodroot. These were the lasting pillars of the Laithe estate.'

"I close with a few acknowledgements for the following officials of the court..."

I couldn't believe the words were my own. But the date at the top of the article was correct; the reporters must have run straight to the presses after my address concluded. I feared for my own mind, not only from the connotations of the words and the vernacular I had used, but far more from the recesses of whatever fugue state possessed me to have forgotten those profound moments of the speech. I knew I had announced my retirement—that much was true. *But why had I no recollection of this 'call to action,' as I had put it, from The Captain?*

Yet there it was in front of me, the newspaper, spread out on the coffee table in the living room of the Laithe family estate, opened to the melodramatic closing statement of my address. In the mystery of my own responses to the reporter's questions, I could hear myself straining with religious zeal, such as a follower making a pilgrimage to the sacred land assumes his own paramount importance.

Reverend Milton surely would have told me to rest, to take off the load I was bearing on my shoulders and protect my weary soul; but no matter how pointed this advice may have seemed, I found the cause more pressing to stop the Laithes's bleeding, which had begun in incremental degrees at Philmore's untimely death and only momentarily been clotted by the recent news of Jacqueline's remarriage. It was ultimately to that end that I found myself in the estate that evening—to quiet my unflagging fervor. Until I confirmed the validity of the new arrangement, I could not rest.

As written in The Captain's will, the estate now belonged to Benton, but in his mental condition I had to ensure that the affairs of the family were documented with proper care. And according to the excerpt from the paper, I had reason to be cautious around the men and women of Newburg who believed my practice to have been corruptly capitalizing on the gains of Benton 'Brier' Laithe, and even Philmore's widow, Ms. Jacqueline Andrews.

What was even more peculiar was the recalled phrase from Roger Laithe—The Captain, excuse me—which surprised me when I read it, as if I had summoned the words from a stowed corner of my subconscious. For it sounded familiar, like the transient resonance of a certain bell in a church tower from the town of one's youth—echoing with terrible solitude, or else malevolent predominance: "in all the land, there were three things to remember…" The three words had come to me from a length of time rather than displacement; it was not distance that separated me from them. *No.* I had been in that very place when I had heard them last. Right there, in that same estate, at a time when there were women's faces seen in drawing rooms, and the walls resounded with the presence of the young. It had been during the season—*Yes!*—that I had taken up counsel for The Captain, when I first heard the three. I thought on them for a while: *Brier, Barren, Bloodroot.*

The last was the easiest to start with, for not 20 paces from where I sat, beyond the arching planes of glass in the windowed foyer, I could make out, just barely in the fading light of the late-August day, the garden beside the path which had bloomed with bloodroot only months before. The flower was indeed significant to The Captain, for what reason was unknown but unnecessary to know—it simply mattered that the garden be kept alive after he passed. Jacqueline had been the one to keep up with it, and judging by the excavated ground and the sweet-earth smell of freshly picked flowers, I believed that the blossoms were adorning the many vases around the house.

My moment of reflection was soon drowned out by the torrent of noise coming from the backyard. I strained to get up from the couch and walk to the screen door, but was hesitant to watch Benton at his craft out of fear that seeing the actions of the man-child moving an iron rod with glass on one end against the steel rollers—producing the terrible scraping noise of metal on metal—would actually make the sound more horrendous. The curiosity, however, made me surrender and stare at Benton while he worked his glass at the crucible, as he had done time and time again since his oldest brother's passing.

To my relief, as soon as I had reached the window to watch the man who had let me inside his estate—for it was Benton's now, without so much as a question—he had moved on from using the punty rod and was sitting at the anvil. I saw his scarred hands, so small that they might have belonged to a boy if not for the roughness of them, and looked intently as he glided the marver smoothly over the iron with the glass bulb taking shape on one end. There was something graceful in each movement. I thought of the first word of the phrase. For it was a Brier before me—somehow both brute and reserved—but still I had not associated it with any allusion that would bring me closer to understanding the other shrouded words or its significance among them.

I knew I must go into her room then, despite the darkness I noticed within. I stopped at the threshold and opened the door slowly, as a tomb raider opens a crypt from which demented spirits might issue forth. I peered into the room and saw a figure moving back and forth through the dark, but I heard no footsteps within nor any shrieks from a possessed soul. I only saw Jacqueline swaying in the rocking chair, which made a subtle splintering noise from the legs against the wood floor. I knew not how to speak to her—this woman who was still grieving the death of the husband she lost two years ago.

It was an empty, myopic voice coming from the widow's mouth that told me I must leave at once. I was startled by her; the croaking voice sounded like a flute out of tune, and I endeavored to leave, when I thought of one thing I could not go without asking—the reason I had come all this way and wished to speak to her.

"I will," I said. "I'm sorry, but Jacqueline, before I go, do you have the papers?"

She made a lethargic attempt at speech and lost a spittle of saliva; the reply came through as a waterlogged noise—as one sounds whose tear ducts have been stopped up from overuse—and she managed to produce the word "book" with scarcely perceptible resolution. I returned to the shelf I had glimpsed before from the couch in the living room, and was rejuvenated with purpose. My fingers traced the spine of book and novel and essay, not once finding what I had come for; until, on one of the last shelves, rested a thin portfolio wedged between two illustrated works. The portfolio was black but had a clear cover, and it showed the marriage certificate of Benton and Jacqueline Laithe—made official in the eye of one witness and one ordained minister, Reverend Milton, announcing a marital union in the power vested by the state of Missouri. It was this document which I had sought to retrieve for my own records, in order to preserve the family's inheritance and to ensure the paperwork would be properly kept by the Laithes's new attorney. Jacqueline even requested that I validate their marriage and said she trusted me no matter my new calling. I told the widow it was not as her lawyer, but as her friend, that I would see it through.

I rested my forearms on my knees and remained squatted, tracing over the remaining spines of the books with my finger and enjoying a resolute peace of mind. I saw one cover that stood out to me, so I took it out of the shelf. 'Missouri Landscapes and Wildflowers' showed in bold silver lettering on the spine; the cover was plain except for the title printed again and set against a forest green sleeve. I remembered this book from The Captain's library. It was a picture book of various flora from the surrounding landscapes with captions underneath each image. There were pages with bent corners and the edges of the covers were frayed from use. I thumbed through the pages and stopped at the first bent corner, which opened to 'Brier'. It read: "Dog rose (*Rosa canina*) and sweet Brier rose (*Rosa rubiginosa*) are spiny perennial shrubs that form dense impenetrable thickets. Both are highly unpalatable to stock and out-compete native vegetation."

I thought of the phrase, of course. It seemed there could be a relation—I felt the same zeal returning which I had grown wary of clouding my senses again, but I could not stop on the cusp of something. So what was it: *that a Brier must be protected, or that it must be weeded out among the neighboring life to preserve the others around it?* I became maddened with the drum of my thoughts unaccompanied by progress, and set the issue down on the coffee table. My head filled with the hollow recollections of old seasons and even older graves that had been dug and filled and covered by new seasons. I thought of The Captain and I thought of my own family. I thought of my child who was my pride, and my brother who had no wife and no heirs. I heard Benton outside again, toiling in the backyard. It was all I could do not to leave—I felt I had to see Jedediah once more to know the estate would be preserved—but I left anyway.

A van sat at the bottom of the drive, pushed to the side where the roots of the trees burrowed into the dry embankment. Two of the van's wheels straddled the slope of the retention basin on the leeward side of the driveway, nudging the half-exposed roots of the trees, and the other two wheels almost tipped up off the ground on the near side, forcing the axle to bear the load of the van and whatever else had been stored inside to make it squat so low.

The leaves were wet with old rain. You could smell it but not see it; nothing could be seen through the darkness, except headlights from far off now, shining through the trees. They came closer and turned as a truck followed the bend of the drive where it met the road coming out of Newburg. For just a moment, the beams of light shot through the stands of trees and lit up the van. It was almost a physical propulsion toward that light that drew me off the porch, toward the bottom of the hill. The beams were the headlights of Jed's truck.

I took each step with care, but couldn't stop my momentum down the steep decline. My legs overtook the body; my mind felt suspended on the single phrase from before. It reached its own pitch against the resonant sound of Benton scoring metal, and ushered a blunt-edged frequency from the crucible range at the top of the hill. I became frantic. I was upset by the many stimulants, by The Captain's voice still in my ear, and Jed approaching fast now, that I nearly fell halfway down the drive. I felt as though there was something slipping past my conscience—something to tell Jed. I had built up to a jog by now, with my legs still in control, but my arms started waving in the air to signal him to slow down.

I cannot fully remember what happened that night—what I said to Jed. I was not sure of myself, but I was not confident enough to divert my course either. I saw Jedediah's truck in full view now, passing the van which leaned awkwardly on its differential and nearly passing me until my flaunting made him stop. I believe it was I who halted him, but as I said, there is much I cannot remember. Regardless, I had an exchange with him that would have little bearing on the tragedy of the Laithes that night. That is to say, I was helpless to stop the course of the family's destiny.

Jedediah moved on up the drive after we spoke, leaving me behind, and for a few restful moments I was satisfied that I had done a true and honest thing. I was a noble man again, and I had already forgotten what that felt like from my practice. I guess I was struggling to find contentment outside of the courtroom, the only discipline I had known for nearly 20 years.

I met with a classmate and colleague of mine the following day who also ended his practice recently; it was Paul. The same lapdog Paul my father had always lauded so much. I could still hear my old man. *Smart kid. Smart enough to know the right path.*

Paul told me he had never felt better than the day he shut the books, and "Really, Dean," he said. "I get it. How can a good attorney not feel lousy when he tries something different?"

He meant good by it, it just felt like bad timing. Terribly bad. There was still so much to do, like worrying about the community, and who would be the next attorney for the Laithes—for I truly put that responsibility on my own shoulders—and most importantly, if this new face could possibly handle their affairs and do them justice without knowing the history. You see, many lawyers never gave their own good and honest try at something. It was probably why they ended up doing something else—*like Paul*—I thought.

He had become a public speaker now, or something. Not all of what he said registered with me that morning, but a few ideas did. He said one thing that I resolved to write about; so now I share it, though it may be years too late, in order to give myself freedom from my own guilt about the events of that night. This is my release.

Paul rolled a toothpick between his fingers like he was bringing fire to kindle, then absentmindedly tucked it out of view. It sat perched behind his left ear as he spoke.

"So you retired," Paul said. "You admitted you were in over your head. Who hasn't been?"

"Well, that's not all," I said.

"No, there's always something else," he said. "Do you remember April 10, 1970?"

"Not the day, but the general context—sure." I said. "I can think of what I would have been doing; where I lived at the time. But the day...not the slightest clue." My throat got chalky talking about time this way. Paul wasn't speaking up so I figured he wanted me to give it a shot.

"April 10 might have been when I brought my last case to probate court, before representing the Laithes," I said. "Maybe that evening I sang to my wife's stomach when she could barely get out of the bathtub. Or possibly it was the night I buried my father down in Salem."

"I was talking about the day the Beatles broke up," Paul said.

"Piss off, Paul," I said. I was irritated.

"You just proved my point exactly."

"What are you talking about?"

"You just recalled all of that beauty, all of that life, and all I remembered was a Lennon interview," Paul said, his eyes grew larger and wet; his voice was leaning forward out of his throat.

"You see, Dean? Just now, there was an entire journey glimpsed in seasons. Swathes of time etched in stories."

"And what is a calendar for, if not the future?" he continued. "It certainly shouldn't be used for the past! Dates and numbers don't matter one bit, Dean, and neither does the time we wish we could get back."

"Paul..."

"There is something I say at most of my conventions when I lead discussions about enabling growth through our mental orientation," he said, taking a short breath but coming back from it quick. "It goes: 'Tomorrow is Yesterday.' Now, think about it..."

"Tomorrow is Today." I interrupted him. I felt cynical and unmoved by the rhetoric. "You were close, though," I said. "Still never pegged you for a Joel fan." I thought I had him; he was aggravated now.

"No," he said, "I know the song. Listen to me, Dean. Hear me straight and give it a chance. Mine is a three-word sentence with three different tenses. You can jumble it up, throw a lot of different words at it, but I've found it most effective just like that."

"Wait a minute, Paul..."

"Are you willing to accept that the worries we once had about the future—the future that is now simply our present—do not suit us anymore?" he said. Paul's eyes were 8 balls now. There was light even in the black parts, but he noticed I was getting tight about something so he kept going.

"There are too many of us who practiced law and will never look ahead of ourselves again, only backward, after we leave the courtroom. That's dangerous, and it's because we're scared of what's next!" He finished.

"Paul," I said. "Can we cut the rest out and talk like we are older men who have seen things and lived them too?"

He shifted in his seat, pushing his mug to the edge of the table, and nodded to the waitress. Paul said, "Okay, okay," and looked at me as a hand flew in from the side and filled his cup back to full. He was waiting for me to start.

"I've been thinking on things."

"Sure," his eyes said. "What things?"

"That we were at a ripe age once but we lost it somewhere," I said.

"You don't mean..."

"More than ever." I said. And I let it all go now:

"We were at an age once when people still asked us where we were from, and where we were headed. And we still had an edge." I paused, and saw him unsheathing his voice.

"But, Dean, you're seeing it all wrong. We never got blunt from use or bent from misuse; the world is still rolled out before us. Nothing is a matter of if but how." Paul said.

"There are some that have surpassed us and some that went before, but our youth is still before us."

And now I decided I would take out my ace. I would lay this game to rest. It wasn't fair, but I had been sitting on it, wondering when to use it for some time now. So I began, and didn't worry about how to counter him. I knew already that his offense had been disarmed, his pride shackled by my shame.

"Now all of life is about where we came from. For the fruit has been picked, and it is not a question of ripeness anymore but a discussion of when it will go bad. And the old can't participate in this mystery, for they have already gone before us and died—so now we, the young, can only gather together and talk about when exactly we lost our youth." I said.

I ruminated later on some other ways I could have ended our conversation. I could have said something that he would have never understood, like "Brier, Barren, Bloodroot." But I felt too sober to be thinking about that again, seeing the pictures in my head from the book and the stone house with its strong timbers shrouded in darkness. I knew, surely, I would need to check on the family again, but it would need to be a long time from then. Yet there was one more matter of legality that I scribbled in the margin of my journal after Paul left that day, which I will copy down now in order to maintain a semblance of my purpose despite all this personal narrative. It was the order of succession that the estate would pass through. It is written:

[The following assumes that the mentioned party has maintained residence in the estate for a minimum of 7 years: Benton Brier is co-owner with Jacqueline—Mrs. Jacqueline Laithe, that is, for it must be that married name, else she could not have been eligible for marital co-ownership as outlined in The Captain's will—to be followed by Jedediah Laithe in the event of Benton's death, and thus relinquishing Jacqueline's co-ownership (the will holds that any *wife*, not *widow*, has the right to co-ownership); and in the event of Jedediah's passing, the inheritance shall be given to the oldest remaining heir of Philmore, Benton, or Jedediah Laithe. In the case of no living heirs, or an heir's untimely death or cognitive incapability, the widow of the firstborn would assume ownership—if and only if the widowed party has remained in the estate since their spouse's passing.]

Jedediah

See, it took me a bit to figure her. Now I know she's about half union, half confederate. And that's the Compromise to thank—made her what they call a "slave state" to appease the South. But she was Yankee through and through in the North. I always thought it strange to make a whole state a slave one, anyway. It was like calling the whole ocean polluted 'cause o' one barrel of oil. She wasn't a real slave state anyhow, but the bill made her one true; so the folks divided her by the Frisco tracks so they didn't have to draw lines in the sand.

In Newburg in middle Miss'ura the Little Piney cuts through the lan' like a knife. It twists around the hills and drops in over the Gasconade, and the river flows through the valley clean out to the Osage Fork.

I yelled out over the pasture: "Sook, cows! Sook!" And that's all it took for 'em to start lookin' over the hills for where the sound was comin' from. "Sook, cows! Sook!" I yelled.

I said it the second time for good measure, but the ground started to shake 'fore long. I was holding the fence open with one hand and groundin' the wire with the other. And there they came. A herd of fifty fine lookin' steers and a handful o' cows heading my way in a wide line like they knew what time it was—'cause they sure did. It was feedin' hour. Only took a short while for those cattle to graze a pasture 'fore they started thinking on a greener one. Made me chuckle. People weren't a whole lot different than them after all.

See, it was a cryin' shame when you had to learn from animals and not your kin 'cause you were born into a family with more wealth than wisdom and not a spitball's guess as to what to do with it. But I figured Jackie might know, with her new marriage and her new ideas, so I just kept watchin' the cattle press the weeds down with their hooves, the herd sweeping in a wide berth now—slowly becoming more of a mass than a line and reachin' the edge of the pasture I was about to set 'em loose in.

Weren't many o' these farms left, I reckoned. *Not like this*—where the lan' was left alone to get fat on its own stores, and the grass left to grow where the sun touched it in the afternoons so completely—so squarely, I'd say—as to raise up big stalks of wild flower and clods o' grass that the cows were all eager to chew to bits, tucking mouthfuls of earth in the clefts of their jowls so they could keep their teeth free to chew the cud. Somethin' 'bout it was right magic, I tell you, seeing the lan' get trodden and dyin' in a way that was right for its renewal. That was the way my ol' man said it anyway: "The earth had to die in places so it could live in others," and: "the worst sin of all was when man chose where it lived and where it died." And boy was he right.

Big farms wouldn't know the lan' if it hit the owners in the mouth; never mind that they reaped a bountiful harvest like our Lord promised to those that were good and faithful. The river took what man thought right for the pasture and the ground died under it. He sprayed the ground with nitrogen, thinkin' that's what it wanted, but not long after you'd see if you went downriver—a ranch hand running to the door of the tenant shoutin' "Bloody murder, there's a curse!" and pointin' at the basin all flooded over. The owner'd come out to inspect the damage and, behold, right yonder he'd see the tips of the leaves o' cabbage breaking the surface of the water, all shriveled and brown. Surely what he saw was the runoff o' that nitrogen killin' all his crop. Now I was no preacher, but there were laws I remembered. Some came from the good book and others from The Cap'n, and the ones I didn't hear from the ol' man I got through Phil. He told me that "givin' nitrogen to the lan' was like givin' water to a fish." What he meant was, it already made enough on its own if you farmed her the right way—no sense in puttin' more down.

But I didn't curse them, 'cause that was the Lord's work, and he knew I weren't no saint neither. I couldn't even say I was a farmer till 'bout two years ago when ol' Phil passed away, 'cause I had no lan' under my name. And with due respect for the law, I suppose I still had no rightful claim to it with ol' Benton still kickin' like he was. That meant I was still just a hand.

I was just a hand even though I was the only Laithe left other'n Harmony, with Benton using that dummy name o' his. And what did he gain from it, since he was reapin' all the benefits of the Laithes but callin' himself a Brier just 'cause his daddy knocked up one and didn't want nobody to know? Last time I checked, The Cap'n was dead and Mr. Brier just as good as, so why should Ben be a Brier? Maybe it broke the curse on him and brought him a wife. See, some called that marriage blessed, but there weren't nothin' righteous 'bout it, I'll tell you. 'Cause who was it other'n me that went to check on how ol' Jackie was doin' all alone in that house? That unwidowed widow, alone with no sound but the awful scrapin' noise coming from Benton rollin' hot glass from the crucible against the rails with the punty.

If you watched folks long enough you saw how they got stuck in their ways—how they called the lan' by a different name dependin' who you asked. See, you had the few who bled on it and cried on it, the ones who cursed it, and the handful that rose from the lan' to gather their daily bread from its dust—and they called it Miss'ura. Then you had folks like Jackie who left it for a time to go to a place that was all smoke 'n sand, where devils and witches came together and stomped out the name o' God from their lan' till his face was nowhere in it. But what was funny: ol' Jackie was from Miss'ura, but she had lived in the devil's desert long enough that when she came back to God's country she couldn't remember what it looked like—much less what it was called—so she blended in with the folks who hadn't ever shed a tear on the lan'. And they called it Miss'uree.

Now all the cattle were through the fence and I took my grabber off the wire. I closed the fence most of the way, leavin' it open a piece as I passed over the pasture one more time. I did this 'cause there were some cows that stuck back in defiance o' what they knew was good for 'em. Maybe they found some little patch of shade and loved it so much they didn't want to risk the nicer pasture a stone's throw away. And sure enough, I found one sittin' down right on the boundary o' the woods where the trees stretched overhead. She looked at me. Her ears twitched and it was like I was the only one left in the world to 'er. I got behind and shoved by the tenderloins.

"Sook cow, Sook!" I said, so that she'd know anytime I yelled it I had somethin' better for her in mind.

I stood watching the sun lay down like a dog in the grass and the last one go through the open fence. It was pretty, no doubt, but all I could think of was Jackie needed checkin' on in that large and lonely house. I started to double back so's to beat the sun to bed, walking right past the chicken coop which needed movin'—it would have to wait till morning—and fired up the Kubota. It was 'posed to be a scorcher that day but it never got higher than seventy. The rain came when it was still light and soaked everything through. Tomorrow'd be a dog's day in hell, I could tell you now. The heat rose and the berries hung fat on their branches. And the world was ripe in the August light with me comin' home to my dead brother's widow and my other brother's wife.

Jacqueline was a good woman, but I was only half as good as Phil and Phil was twice the man The Cap'n was, so that put me about eye to eye with my pops, more or less. I missed Philmore. I gave him my word I'd look after Jackie when I could tell the coal had already gotten to his lungs. It only took a few weeks after a bad blowout in the mines that took several men for his light to go out—he inhaled so many poisons, it's a wonder he even made it a month. But he took it true, without much pain, and I couldn't resent him none after I gave him my word that I'd take care o' his ol' lady for him. I told Phil if he could stick around long enough, he'd "see those pastures grow till they were high as my knees." He laughed at that.

I guess I was right even though he weren't around to see it. I could hardly see my truck between the reeds along the creek bed that'd grown taller than me, hidin' away my red, vintage gal parked up on the ridge overlooking the Osage valley. The sun was skinny dippin' now; the black lan' under the horizon undressed her, takin' her top off till you looked long enough for the sun spots to show. I stepped on the gas and the Kubota purred all the way up the hill 'fore I came to a stop and killed the engine. It was all I could do not to look back at the rollin' swells of the Ozark steppes, even with Jackie waitin' on me, but I couldn't help it.

I looked out at the meadows and the foothills, seeing the young lan' and rememberin' when it was just dirt. Unlivable. Animals came to those pastures before and thought nothing o' the ground. And then my brother, Philmore—*God be good to him*—knelt down in the dirt and crumbled the balls of soot in his hands and saw what the lan' was before it was. It gave him somethin' to aim for—and what man didn't need that? He toiled and labored over that lan' for the rest o' life; Jackie almost hadn't a choice in it, but she was good to him anyway. She was a good woman and a good wife. Only strike against her was she couldn't give him a child.

I threw the toolbox in the back of my truck and fired her up. It was a good drive. The road snaked through the woods and the trees threw dark shapes against the sky. I drove right on through town and glimpsed the lights on Main, the hole-in-the-wall theater on the end and the bar slouched on its corner before the road climbed into the hills. Soon I made it to the house and saw Harmony's van as I turned into the drive.

One of the best things I ever did was take the engine out o' that thing. Now Harmony couldn't go nowhere and I could keep an eye on her better so the eyes o' the family didn't get to her first. And they would, I told her. I lost a brother, took care o' his wife even when she married Ben, and got a daughter out of it that I loved more than the world. I looked on Harmony as a kind o' light; or maybe she was the switch that turned it on—reckon I didn't know. But I could feel the world at my heels accusing me of oversteppin' my bounds with that girl. It was strange, considerin' Harmony'd been in my care as long as she was in Phil's until his death, that folks were still out for me. All I knew was that that girl was the fruit o' Phil's lovin' years, and that she was gone with her mother till she showed up out o' the blue, with Phil only two years away from dyin' and herself already close to womanhood.

Harmony didn't know I loved her like my own daughter, 'cause I'd never tell her. Tellin' her'd make it good as law, and the only law a ranch hand could count on was the lan'. So I let Harmony know it unofficial by keepin' an eye out for her and chasing away all those no-goods, them hell-raisin' boys. Besides, she had a good friend Addie who kept her safe too—and speaking o' the devil if it wasn't one o' those worse-than-sin boys coming this'a ways down the drive soon as I turned in, flailing and yellin' all kinds o' noise and pointing at the house on top o' the hill.

It only made it worse as soon as I saw the outline o' the figure and saw that it was none other than the lawyer—not some prick kid—makin' a scene under the sound of the awful *score, score, score* o' the punty rod glidin' against the metal at the range behind the house. Benton worked it hard, making the iron scream and brewin' up a proclamation fit for the second comin' o' Christ. And now Dean was making a raucous of his own, hollerin' and waving me down to stop.

"Get, get!" I said. "And don't come back. What business you got here anymore, now that Phil's gone two years in the grave?" I said.

Dean was in an outrage. He walked to Harmony's van and used it to talk, writing a phrase in the fog on the windows. It was a list of three. He wrote all three down and circled the second.

"Barren, barren!" he said to me, madder'n a wet hen, peckin' his finger back up at the estate blackened by the night but softly brightened by the glow of the range out back. Benton was still raisin' hell on the glass. It flared louder every second, so I raised my voice and strong-armed it against Dean.

"Who's mystery is that other than yours? We know all about Jacqueline, and that ain't your fight, you ol' court clown. Quit raisin' hell—or did you not hear me? I said, get!"

"Barren," he said. "All down the line. Barren."

He wasn't makin' any sense to me anymore. I caught him saying Benton's name under his breath: "Brier. He's a Brier—but what is Bloodroot...what does it mean?!" Pointing up the hill toward the howlin' furnace and the whistling from the glass being blown in the backyard. It was like a shell of sound, fillin' itself up as soon as it hollowed out. I was out of the truck now, telling Dean Elliot he oughta be in the can with the other folks he used to represent for his blatant trespassin'. I shook the dust off'a one o' my shoes and told him where I'd put the other one if he didn't turn and get off my property. He left, sure enough. I didn't even bother to go up to Harmony in her van and see if she was alright. *Some protector, I was.*

I think it was that sound—awful as death—echoing through the valley and beatin' against my chest like a hammer. I had to check on Jacqueline.

Harmony

The way she was digging, you'd think she was looking for buried treasure. I was clenching the mattress and looking away—always away, never at her.

If I had the energy, I would've made a list of all the things you should know if you were a young girl growing up with a stepmom who locked herself up in a dark room all the livelong day. I bet I could even knock out a couple right now. First on the list:

1. *Never let your partner expect your pleasure.*

It took me too long to come up with that one. Not the feeling, but the thought with the words and all. Sometimes words didn't flow nice but you had to sit with them till they came. Reminded me of the phrase "to be a lake and not a river." Reverend Milton said that to me once and I wonder if it took as long for him to come up with as my line. Anyway, what he meant was that lakes just take the water and store it up; rivers move it. All you had to do was store water and let the Lord move it. I was trying to obey the old preacher, but I reckon I had committed a sin by faking my pleasure for Addie. She just kept digging in there for her treasure that wouldn't come.

My insides dried up a while back and I didn't know why or when exactly it happened. I was supposed to be like a well, but the spring came and no water got drawn with the pail, so I sat there in our van and became a lake for Addie because she was being something else. It was starting to hurt, her touching my spot till it was raw, but she had the idea I liked it. And maybe I did for a time, the attention at least, so I guess the real fault was when I told her she could expect me to want it—of course that was before I ever made the rule.

Jacqueline tried to be a real mama to me, but she let herself get in the way. All it took was a woman who couldn't have children herself and a young girl like me coming around after my birth mom died, and Jackie's greed took it from there. I kept looking up that drive at the house, darkened and black against the faint dusk, and thought of Jacqueline in her room without any light coming in at all. And then came Uncle Jed in his truck blowing exhaust and driving up to her dog-like and loyal.

It didn't seem right to me for a man to check on another man's wife like that. Benton couldn't do a thing, though. He had no say even in his own marriage. What a day he must've had when he was, no doubt, hunched at the crucible and minding his business when he learned he was to be married. But that still wasn't enough to stop him from invading everyone's air with the metal-on-metal concert of sound that the range took and distributed to the vales of the river basin.

Boy, listen to that! I could see a thing and make it sound nice, couldn't I? That was Jackie to thank, but I'll get

to that. After she married Benton without his say in it—
dragging him to the Phelps County Courthouse and meeting
Reverend Milton to officiate the union—she stepped right in
to become the second Laithe wife, a successor to herself, as if
the quicker return to normalcy would grant a swifter
bludgeon to her sorrow. Let me tell you what; you could
speed up a clot to the body, but you couldn't hurry a
wounded soul. I guess I just saw things clearer since I was
dealt a dead dad and a good-as-dead mom. Sure, it was still a
scar for me—my daddy dying—but he didn't drag it on like
she did. He was just gone and there was nothing more to it.

Now, earlier, when I pointed out my way with
language, that was on behalf of Jackie trying to make me a
writer before I ever wanted to be. She thought I could
channel her grief for her, and so made it my job to wrap the
tourniquet around the wound that my dad left behind. Even
still, she had only just begun the process that was delayed
nearly two years, by grieving my dead father and shutting
herself up in that dark-as-night corner room of our estate.
What a shame, too! Beyond her blackened window, hung
with heavy drapes, there was the best view in all of
Newburg, looking out over the river valley and seeing the
Little Piney twist and turn all through the rippled land. The
hill country was never as beautiful as it was there in early
fall—it could have inspired anyone to write.

But writing was bittersweet for me. I often felt a
desolation in my heart even when I found the words, as if

they manifested Jackie's vengeance for never having finished that novel of hers. I wish writing made me feel better, but it didn't. And I never got a chance at doing it for myself, so I stuck to deepening the language of the heart—a language that didn't live on words but on love for my soul's sweet secret, Adelaide, whom I loved with all of me. She was kind and pure and good, but at that moment she didn't know that it was high time that she quit digging in me for treasure or pleasure or whatever it was that would never come.

And who showed up, right as my Uncle Jed was passing by in his truck, other than that awful man I had always tied with death? Why, *it was Dean Elliot!* He was making gestures and signs with his hands. He was yelling something too, but his words couldn't cut through the loudness that hung in the air from Benton's glasswork piercing through. I could barely make out what Dean was yammering about, but there was Uncle Jed in his truck shooing the deranged attorney off our property. That was when I saw Dean do something strange. He came over to our van, and put his finger to the window, writing in the layer of condensation, the words: 'Brier, Barren, Bloodroot'. He circled the second, then pointed up to the house where Jackie was. I seized up as if a bright light had shined on me, with Addie lying by my side comforting me—her arms around my chest as my whole body shuddered.

There was something horrible revealed in that word. Something set in motion long ago and seen in latent ways—

like my blood that never came till much later than the end of my adolescence, when my real mom was dead or gone or dead *and* gone, and I had to mark my womanhood by other signs. Jackie was no help with this either, since she was preoccupied denying grief in all its forms. Nevertheless, she found out long ago she would never have children; and now Dean, with his muffled shouting through the van door, was talking about a barrenness that had haunted the Laithes for years now, out of fear that there would be no more heirs for the estate one day. And despite my general discomfort around men, the pressure was already starting to fall on me to have a child who would be this Laithe Messiah. So I'll add a rule to the list:

2.   *Don't trust a promise unless it has seven colors.*

My father promised me I would find a good man one day and that I would have a handful of children. "More than you'll know what to do with, Harmony." he said. If he had only lived a year or two longer, maybe I would've told him I didn't want a man anyway—so it wouldn't matter if I couldn't give him any grandchildren. Besides, I found more comfort in Adelaide, who was reminding me now and taking me in her arms again. She knew I was startled by the yelling outside our little home, and said "it's alright, it's alright, sweet lovely." It was nice for her to call me that.

A small twitch escaped the corner of her mouth. I looked up at her—feeling so safe all of a sudden—and wanted to bury myself in her comfort. But things couldn't be savored completely every time. I couldn't track down that twitch of her lips or where it went, so I tucked it in my soul instead. Finally, hearing that Dean was gone and we had some quiet again, I kissed her true and got above her so that she sank into the mattress. My hair fell down and around her face. She felt like mine.

"My innocent Adelaide," I said, "Let me make love to you and then I'll go across the river."

We made it together and I took the sweetness from her like a drug, hanging it over my thoughts so that they sounded poetic once more. I saw the world around me in color again.

Afterward it was getting dark outside, but even the night had shades. I knew the feeling couldn't last forever, like a painter relishing her palette of deep mauves and bold indigos knows they cannot be recreated, so I made use of my own colors and let them paint everything I saw.

Out in the late-evening air, the aftermath of summer humidity left no dryness anywhere. Each rock did shine, and river bed turned to river run. Ivy colonized the fallen timbers, showing a residue of the wet invading it. The droplets in the air married the dew leftover from morning, and the leaves of the trees were crying. My name was spelled everywhere for me: Harmony, Harmony, Harmony. A lump swelled in my throat.

I walked along the path that ran perpendicular to the road, away from home, and stumbled on a rock crossing the Piney. The blood from the scrape made my leg wet like all the things around me and touching me. I thought I must be cursed, and after Dean's peculiarities I felt an apathy— maybe even a nihilism.

The meeting place was always the same. Sometimes my cousin Andy would be there, sometimes he would just leave the baggie; but he knew where to collect my money anyway so it didn't matter all too much. The drop was in the nook of a split stone on a small footbridge that had crumbled into the river a long time ago. The remains of the bridge had been untouched for as long as I had been alive. Large pieces of stone lay in the stream, like miniature versions of the elephant rocks out in Iron County, near Johnson's Shut-Ins, where the East Fork of Black River trudged past the Ozark trail and tumbled clumsily past gigantic boulders set on the shoulder of the Reynolds County Line. I went to the Shut-Ins in my head every time I crossed this section of the Piney and saw the stones disrupting the current in different places, forming a network of their own.

With the baggie in my hand, I turned back to climb the debris of rock to our side of the river, when I heard, still invading the evening air like a solitary trumpet, the rhythmic scraping pattern of Benton working his rod against the rollers. There were breaks, of course, for the amount of time it took him to feed the glass through the glory hole and reheat it; then the rolling on the rails again; the setting of the glass with the jacks; and finally, the angled tempering on the anvil—forcible as the wind but able to charge ahead, as if the sound came first and then the blowing force behind it.

I crumpled up the top of the bag and used my flashlight the rest of the way. There was no light in the sky, only a kind of afterlight which had been cauterized by the day and left to cool just beyond the hills. In front of me, the estate was barely silhouetted against the pulverized light of the furnace blaring up behind the house.

The fire under the crucible changed the quality of the air as well. The heat rose. It never came down the hill to Adelaide and me, but it must have consumed Benton. I could never understand the worth of that glasswork to him. No doubt, he was dealt a worse hand than the rest of us, for there was a way that war split a man's personality in two; not neatly either, as if it were perforated down the middle, but instead with torn edges and splayed corners. Benton was the glass and the war was the rod, keeping him hanging over the rails, just barely on the precipice of death. The gunshots were the glass clamps, and the redness of the sky changed the air around him, pinning him down on the metal rollers while he was still pliable—while he still had give from the heat of the crucible.

I felt pain, thinking of my uncle like that, and it wasn't even my own pain to bear. I clenched the bag under my arm and understood a lot about Addie all of a sudden but nothing about Benton, since I couldn't bear the cross he carried with him everywhere. I felt two drops of water fall onto my wrist, and held my hand out to see if a night rain was settling in. There was nothing.

My eyes felt hazy, swollen with water in them. I blinked it away just enough to see the moon's afterglow illuminate the van through the trees.

"My sweet," I said out loud. "I'll be there soon. And I'm going with you this time."

I pulled aside a row of cattails and walked toward the van in the darkness.

Jedediah

Benton's glasswork could'a been heard over a coyote in a trash compactor. And the quality wasn't much prettier than that neither.

I made my way up the drive. The flowers were gone from the side of the gravel path. Jackie picked the garden clean a while back, but since I was still livin' on the ranch this was my first time being at the estate and seein' them gone. Why their leavin' made me feel bad, I didn't know—after all, she'd gathered them up in, say, April, so they could last through the summer. When you picked them was a science, and when you cut them was important too. Plus, Jackie had her own practice of hangin' them upside down by the stems so's they'd keep their color and smell all the way to winter.

I went around the house where I heard Benton making his scrapin' and howlin' noises. I couldn't figure what it was he was making or why it couldn't wait till mornin'. It just *had* to be done while the world was winding down for bed. But I'll say one thing 'bout this night particular—the way the moon was filled up, I already reckoned a fella weren't gonna get as much shut-eye as he got most nights.

I looked through the dark night and saw the light o' the moon and the sparks flyin' this a'way and that over the back o' Ben's shoulder, and I knew I had to do what was best for ol' Jackie in the house who's peace was bein' disturbed. I started yellin' up a storm of my own.

"That's 'nough for now, Ben! Get in, will you? Benton!" I yelled it loud and he must'a noticed, 'cause he stopped on a dime, real smart-like. But Ben didn't let another moment expire 'fore he turned back to the bench and kept moldin' the globe of glass. I saw now it was a bulb he was making; I just wanted to know who for. But prob'ly it weren't none of my business. It weren't *my* wife I had gone up there to check on. It was his'n.

I looked at the stone columns o' the house and watched the wood trellis blow out from against the wall and come crashin' on back. The wind picked up from the valley and bore 'gainst it. Her foundations tightened up, and the back o' the estate fixed its posture now, restin' on its heels and exhalin' the strain at last. I looked at Benton again. He kept workin' it as if he never noticed the gusts o' wind nearly blowing the embers from the glory hole onto him. He had a backbone, that one.

See, Benton was a different man when I knew him before. I was younger once, too; just a kid when he left. And I knew the only way a man got to come back home in the heat of conflict like he did was when his screws got loosened and there was no kick left in him. I'd been around long enough to know what war did to a man. I knew war was your brother needin' help to find clean drawers 'cause he just wet the bed, and you not findin' any 'cause he never went to the store to buy new ones. And it was you havin' to go for your older brother—your 32-year old brother—since you wouldn't let him drive the truck. You couldn't. 'Cause war was the sound of a muffler discharge to a man who was still on the run from the Vietcong. It was a wound bandages couldn't heal. That is, unless you counted a bolt of lightin' sent into his brain from a machine that was supposed to shock the bad memories away. You hoped it would, at least. You hoped it took the bad ones before it shocked away the good. And it made a man revert back to his youth, too. I knew that was what drove Ben to the crucible—pickin' it back up from when he'd learned glassblowing by watchin' The Cap'n. It was one of the few things our ol' man always let Benton come to the estate to watch, tellin' Fanny it was a "life skill that a boy ought to know." We'd sit together, three brothers with no loose screws yet, lookin' on as The Cap'n fastened the clamps to the hot bulb and tempered the surface smooth against the anvil. Ben always wantin' to take over more than Phil or me. And now there I was watchin' him work just like we were kids again—him clearly not hearin' or noticing me. But I felt glad that at least he had something.

I walked into the house from the back, through the screen door, and went toward Jacqueline's room finally. I reckoned she was sittin' in that rocking chair of hers—the one Phil made. I opened the door and saw Jackie now in the moonlight. It was spillin' in from the corners of the window that the curtain couldn't cover. She kept it dark—*death-*

73

dark—I thought. I looked at her and my heart turned and chased itself back into place. It pained me a little to see her hurtin' so. Something strange happened to me as I was about to speak to her; I choked on a word and panicked, then closed the door again to think it through. I rubbed the back o' my neck where my hair grew down long and thought o' Phil and how he would'a done it. I couldn't think how to belong in the room, unless—*unless I had somethin' to show for and give her*. That was good. Now I was thinkin' how Phil would'a done it.

I went into the kitchen, turned on the light, and took out a glass from the cupboard. My eyes were adjusted to the light after the sides of the glass ran with water and I shut 'er off. I must'a not felt well—scared that when I opened Jackie's door again my eyes wouldn't know what darkness was anymore, nor the shapes it took. I waited a bit for my heart to steady from all the turnin' over, then I went through the living room and saw where Dean had been, *no doubt*, sittin' in front of the coffee table with that ol' picture book turned to a white flower and the mornin' paper opened to that story o' him in there.

I couldn't figure why the lawyer, or whatever he called himself now, went rummagin' through our shelf like that. The way he invaded our lives felt like gettin' spoken to when you were nothin' but an inch or two away from a person. And you felt the drops o' spittle hittin' you on the cheek, wonderin' why you couldn't snatch some peace 'n quiet to think 'er over.

I made it back to the hallway and felt a lump swellin' in my throat. I opened the door. Jacqueline was rockin' back and forth in the dark and my heart rolled up the sides of my chest and started skippin' rope with my stomach; everything felt twisted 'round and flutterin'. I knew I'd better get it over with.

"Miss Jackie?" I said, openin' the door wide enough to see a thin line of light streakin' her face. "I got you some water, okay? You doin' alright up here? By yourself all day?"

"I'm okay, Jed," Jacqueline said to me, barely loud enough. "Shut the door when you go, please—it's too much light. I promise, Jed, I don't need anything."

The heartache feelin' was bad when I'd first seen 'er, but honest to God it was nothin' compared to the way her final words hit me then. These hit me square in the trunk like a steel-toed shoe comin' down on a wet log with all its weight. I couldn't remember if I closed the door or not, but before I knew it I was opening another door and shuttin' myself up in the room across the hall to escape the moment, just like a kid.

The bed was little. The wallpaper was old. There was a small lamp that I turned on to see what the smell was coming from. It was the smell of earth and the petals o' the flowers that had been picked. I saw them now: about 20 of them, hung from their stems, upside-down and bunched together—with the color all there. The roots were gone but the faces were white still; a bad eye might have told you they were daises. My hand was on my chest now and I was rubbin' all the pain out—kneading it like it was a big clump o' dough and pushin' the heel of my hand back into my chest. There was no more hurt, but my hand was bruisin' it now from all the kneadin', and I felt it under my skin. I said somethin' soft to myself or someone else now.

"Blame you, Cap'n, for this bad heart o' yourn."

I kneaded the dough a little longer, sittin' on the edge o' the bed. The glass was still in my hand. My eyes squinted a little, my face felt small and wrinkled. I never liked when it felt like that—when the world got smaller around you and you felt it shrink to the size o' the room, and you were bigger than you wanted to be all o' sudden.

There were two small drops o' water or somethin' else that found the water in the glass. It was too dark for me to find out where they came from, even with the lamp on. The clamoring at the range went quiet now. There was nothin' but the wind moving the trellis against the wall and the sound of wood on stone. I heard a screen door open at the back o' the house.

"That you, Ben?" I said through the door, but I don't think he heard me.

Now I just wanted to get out. I wanted to run, light out from there and catch the sunrise hittin' the backs o' the cattle in the pastures. But I didn't dare open the door and have Benton see my face like that. *I couldn't.* So I waited a spell for him to get whatever it was he needed and start blastin' away with the punty rod again.

I heard the footsteps heavy and shuffled—just the way Benton did—so I knew it was him. The wood bent under his boots. The wind rose and swelled, and the tang of faded flowers was in the air all around me. I breathed them in and held myself steady as the mad wind shook the base o' the house. Benton stopped right outside my door. I got all nervous about him findin' me, until I realized it weren't my door he was outside of, but the door across the hall from me. I heard a sound escape his lips. I couldn't make out everything on account o' that hushed and hurried way Benton said anything. All I knew was I could hear him say 'shine' over 'n over again.

"Jack'lin—" just the way he always said it, "have it done for you by next week."

He was sayin' all kinds o' nonsense—almost soundin' like a song—and that weird bit: "Jackie is your wife." *Was he talking to me now? No,* I figured, *that was just the way he spoke.* Started to feel crazy hearin' myself think.

I tensed up from head to toe at the sound that came next. A loud crash, as if a ball o' hail hit the window and shattered it. I sat bolt-upright and listened to the wind. I got out o' my bed to check on them both—about to give up my hiding place in the room across the hall—till I heard Benton cleanin' shards o' glass on the floor without any wind howlin' through an open window. *What was the shatter?*

The sound came from right outside my door. I dared not move so's to let Benton or Jackie know I'd heard the whole thing. I waited near an eternity till Benton's moanin' died down. He was like a hurt dog whimperin'.

I didn't know how long I'd be prisoner that night to ol' Jackie and Ben, so I did a thing for myself I didn't expect. I took off my dirty clothes, put them all in the closet so I couldn't smell the sweat and dirt on them, and opened the window just a slice so's to let the nice cool wind blow through. The angry air died down and a softer breeze settled in real nice.

I started countin' the sheep I had to move in the north pasture the following day, and sooner than I knew it I was countin' sheep I didn't have to move, somewhere in pastures far off, in lands I didn't own and on fields I never had to fence. The cool wind was temperin' the covers like it was the voice o' my mama who I never got to know and prob'ly never would. But I reckoned she was realer than ever to me right then—with my naked body under the covers and my hands moving down between my legs, puttin' my cold fingers between my thighs to make them warm while the other hand warmed under the pillow. All cocoon-like, I laid there, lettin' Mama sing to me while I counted the sheep. And I knew the sun was takin' all the time it needed.

Harmony

"I wrote this for you when you were gone," Adelaide said. "But close the door, baby. That wind's coming in."

"Sing it to me," I said.

"I want to play you the melody and have you sing it back to me," she said.

"I'll sing it for you, sweet. Teach me."

"Okay. The chorus goes:

Darling, where do you go—
when you're an arm's length away?
The ocean's deep;
and my heart is clay.
I'll be here in the morning;
but tonight, I away.

"What do you think?" Adelaide said. She stopped the last note with her hand on the strings, and looked into my eyes. "Baby, don't do that," she said, coming close to me and wrapping her arm around my neck. "Don't do it here."

"There's nothing to cry about tonight," she said.

I rubbed briny water from my face. It was coming from the corners of my eyes—they felt tight and swollen but I felt warm with her near me.

"Look at this bed." she said. "Remember earlier, in this bed? That was ours. Don't cry Harmony; this is the home we share. I love you."

I cried some more but not shaking now, that kind when your chest shrivels up and the ceiling feels high. I didn't care about anything as much as I cared about Adelaide. I wanted to tell her and show her. I wanted to write her a book or at least a poem. There was something our life together had ought to stir in me that I could show her and give her like the song she gave me.

"There are a million ways to say I love you, Addie," I said, with my head turned into her neck, "You just have to know which one I'm choosing. Can you know it and keep it safe for me?" I spoke with a faint voice just loud enough so she could hear. My voice cracked at the end of the question and another tear rolled onto her collar bone. I kissed it away.

"I know which one," she said.

"Let me go with you tonight," I said.

Adelaide picked my head off her neck and held it with both hands. She looked deep into my eyes and wiped the corners with her fingers. "Are you sure?" she said.

"Yes, Addie, I'm sure," I said. "I don't want us to be apart tonight. I don't think I could take one more second away from you."

"Okay, Harmony, but not yet," she said. "You can't be so shaky when you first try it. I know better. Okay?"

I nodded.

I watched her bring her guitar back out and play me our song. I loved the sound her fingers made on the strings when she moved between chords. That sort of scraping squeak. It was my favorite part. There was a lot of that in this song—that's why I loved it.

"It's a simple picking pattern," Addie said.

I smiled. It felt like ours.

My body had stopped shaking so much. I was calmer and felt a lot heavier after the cry; my legs were sunken into the bed. Not even the glassblowing at the top of the hill could bother me. It was peace.

"How are you, baby?" Adelaide said. "No, don't say anything yet. You look calmer—that's good. I love you. Did you know that I love you?"

"Yes, sweet."

"Now, tell me a place you go in your head to feel at ease—totally at ease in all of the world," she said. "Somewhere you have been before."

"Eagles." I said. "Watching eagles with my dad."

"What were they like?"

"They were way up there," I said, pointing my arm toward the low ceiling of the van. "And beautiful. I could pick them out better than any of the hawks or buzzards at Uncle Jed's farm." I paused and saw Adelaide smiling, looking up to where my arm was still raised.

"And my dad always had his binoculars with him. He would say, 'Look Harmony, there, about to land on the perch!', and ever so quietly we watched the great bird land. It was beautiful, Addie. My papa never had to add anything to nature to make it inspiring. He was the perfect scientist."

"That's lovely," Adelaide said.

"I miss him," I said. "I'm sure Jackie does too."

"Do you remember the song I played?"

"Some of it."

"Show me."

I sang her what I remembered.

"Oh, H, you have a terribly pretty voice," she said. "I think you are calmer now. Do you want to try it?"

"Yes."

Adelaide reached for the baggie and leaned her guitar against the head rest of the driver's seat. She took out two syringes, gauze, and a smaller, clear bag. I turned around and found the lighter she always used. There was a flicker of anxiety. I breathed slowly and felt my chest rise and fall, scrunching my toes and pointing them down toward the end of the mattress, then I sat up to see what she was doing. It helped me to visualize; it had always been that way. It was the same with the bird watching. The eagles were mine and my father was mine, at least the version of him in my mind was. It helped to see him in that memory.

I told myself my mom hated my father when I was very young because I never saw him. It worked for a while— I made him an idea and it was safe. Then she brought me to him when I got too expensive to take care of, and he materialized into something. He was more than an idea, and I got him for two years; but when he died to me the second time it hurt more than the first, because it was harder than letting a thought go. *At least now I would always have him in my head. He never died there.* Here was Adelaide with the needle.

"I ought to give it to you first," she said.

I looked up at the ceiling and forgot about it all so that I would have more room to remember how he was. I thought about the way he fell asleep with the radio on after supper and his hands clasped over his belly, and the way he would talk about a band and start humming their songs rather than just telling you straight. My father was the centerpiece of the room and the rest of us were the decor. And it was an occasion to watch him because you knew this was a man who was everything to many people. I reflected on the two years before he left us as the ceiling undressed itself and flew away from me. The mattress and sheets touching me changed. I heard Adelaide and a bubbling sound while she was getting a hit ready for herself. *I'll be here in the morning; but tonight, I away.*

I heard the song again, but it was distorted and strange. The notes came from a long, long way off.

Soon I was relieved of the weight of my grief—I was new. I decided that tomorrow I would tell Jacqueline I forgave her. I'd tell Uncle Jed I was sorry for being so guarded, and I would even take care of Benton while he was away at the farm. Addie could help me. And there was no problem that couldn't be fixed.

I felt myself levitating. The world around me radiated colors as if it had always been dimmed. It was a mesmerizing place.

Jacqueline

What was there in a name? That girl was given one that meant peace and tranquility, and she spoiled it; or maybe it was that she could never live up to it. And she insisted she never wanted children. What a strange—no—what a *shameful* thing to forfeit the only gift God gave a woman. I hated her and mourned my own loss, but only after feigning indifference toward it; so it was there where I found the vice of my long-suffering envy. I had the Little Death in me. The Passover Angel. I never had a chance like Harmony, so now I resented her for the chance she was throwing away. But it was hard to reinforce the bulwarks of my anger, the way I saw Philmore in her eyes.

Just like Harmony I became a woman once, and I could never forget the precious days that came before. I remember soft rains peddling the seeds of wild grass into the Osage River and buds of summer flowers floating in the water. I would row downstream with my father as stalks of crushed reeds drifted lazily by, and steer my canoe out of the rain to rest under a canopy of long-armed trees bowing over the water.

"Missouri weather changes its mind more than a girl changes clothes, Jackie," my dad would say. Using both arms, I covered my head from getting wet from the rain and laughed.

But the age of the Little Death came suddenly; the freshness of youth was sequestered from me during the day, and I grieved the loss of it in the night. One afternoon, encumbered with solitude, I stretched my legs and embarked on a pilgrimage for my womanhood. The roads in Westphalia were uneven from winter rains freezing in the cracks, and I stepped and hobbled over every danger, feeling as though each triumph was fortifying my newfound sensibility. Storefront windows bore the ceiling-gray sky and draped it over St. Joseph's steeple, and I walked into my father's general store to tell him I had become a woman. He was without words.

My dad was everything to me except a mother, and so he gave me no solace in the shrouded temple of his masculinity. I had no one to bear it with me, no one to embrace the age-old ritual that welcomed in the young girls and dismissed them afterwards, having lost one thing and gained another. But alas, in central Missouri, along the banks of its rivers, youth was always slipping.

A childhood spent in the Ozark plateau between Salem and Jefferson City was here one day and gone; such that even those raised up on it did not feel as if they were actually from there. In those days, the land swelled and shifted under the hooves of the cattle and the sun cultivated the ground under the humid August air. Summer broke up the stiffness in the pastures left over from spring, and ushered strong winds into the basin of the Gasconade. In the valley, the weather from the day harbored itself until night, bringing marvelous displays to throw upon the evening sky.

And as an older woman I wondered who could know her like those who had gone down below and knew their land on the other side of death. Those souls, like my father and his before him, must have seen the scarlet clouds tearing the sunset in two—like the ripping of a curtain without finding the seams.

The thick drapes in my room were presently blocking out the light from the moon, and the darkness left the real world no chance to blot out my dreams. Yet still I was unable to reside in the solemnity of my wayward youth any longer. In the darkness of that empty alcove, I ceased finding sleep and ceased trying; for all was sacred to me save the awful rhythm of Benton's crude instruments scraping against metal.

It persisted: *one, two, one, two,* as Benton smoothed the air out of the glass. Surprisingly, the sounds didn't drive me to pieces at first, because I found that occasionally his glasswork was all I had of Phil. Sometimes, on hot days, I stood by the back door and saw the end of Benton's blowpipe dipping into the crucible, and pictured instead the man who once took me into the woods near Eminence and plunged a stick into a wide honeycomb to impress me. That fleeting second where Benton brought the pipe up out of the crucible—before he shaped it with the rod—was the precious second that Phil was still with me, and I remembered how happiness could rise in one's chest.

Hearing the cacophony still bolstered by the wind, it was hard for me to picture anything other than how it truly was. The sun had already set, and my imagination with it. I thought of my typewriter and a far-off dream as my door opened, only a crack, but produced a thin line of light and nothing else before it receded without incident. The lawyer had already left, so it must have been Jed come to check on me again—for I heard the sound of Benton shaping the glass all the while. I felt unnecessarily disturbed then, and a rage against Jedediah welled up in me that had no justification, but continued surging nonetheless. God knows he didn't deserve it in the least, but it was hardly enough to quiet my anger against him for being in the way of my rights to the land—my Philmore's estate and property.

It was as if the covenant between Benton and I wasn't true enough in the eyes of the law; for Jedediah seemed keen on being the last stronghold that I must breach in order to honor Phil and take care of his land. I fortified my mind to withstand the next disturbance from Jed, which was sure to come, and reconciled with him in my heart by believing I would marry him next should something happen to Benton—right on down the line, until I received the land Phil had always wanted me to take care of when he passed. And as though it were a chain of events my own restless thoughts had nurtured, conjuring all that was dreaded into reality, the door again swayed open—only this time wider—and I narrowed my eyes and turned my face away from the torrent of light. The deluge filled the room, and in the negative space of light stood Jedediah with a glass of water in his hand.

He murmured something I could scarcely hear. I dared not turn and look into his face, that face that had been tuned with the chords of a somber scale. I told him something of which I only remember the first and last part. It was my own voice, but it was labored, and felt as though it dissipated against the hard light that kept my face turned away.

"I'm okay, Jed. I don't need anything." I said. His shadow left me; the door gaped open.

I could never marry that man. I thought. *Unless I must.*

I despised him, with his barbarianisms and imposing way of 'taking care' of me. I never held my husband Benton's lack against him, but with Jed it was different. And still, neither one could be Phil for me.

Philmore always made me feel that time was on our side. When we first got married and moved to Eminence in the fall of '71, he said, "We can take as long as we want here," but it was always Newburg where he wanted to settle down. I liked that. I felt agency in our marriage, knowing it would span over multiple places and properties; I saw our lineage not as a large river but as a stream with many tributaries.

My dad's further decline in health only brought me nearer to the reality of death, and although it was burdensome, this grounded me. It turned out to be a brain tumor—the very thing that had caused the stroke on the same day I met Philmore. The doctors determined it inoperable, but mine and Phil's lives didn't change drastically until after the second stroke. We had been married a year by then, and already our days were spent worrying about my father. Phil was my strength even during my constant preoccupation with my dad, and he took the initiative to drive me to St. Louis on the occasion that another episode forced me to come at once and see he was cared for.

I knew we didn't have much time left with him, and this saddened Phil in a way I could not have foreseen—as if his lack of an *honorable* father in his own life was enough of a reason for him to attach himself so profoundly with mine. The two became close in a short amount of time.

I thought of one occasion where Phil had loved my father well and loved me even better, and did reminisce about it on evenings such as that August dusk in '79—the same night as Benton's tragedy—which had now wrapped its dark shawl around my face and hid me from the lighthearted tranquility I once knew. I went to the light of my memories in search of solace.

It was early on in our marriage, shortly after the diagnosis, when Philmore offered to pick me up from the city after driving there by myself to be with my dad. He had had the worst stroke yet; but thankfully, he restored from it and we arranged for him to be on hospice at a center near Jefferson City, closer to family. And as if it were a sign from God days before the scare that sent me tearing up Route 44 to St. Louis, we got a call from Dean Elliot about Philmore's great uncle, Allan Laithe, telling us he had passed away.

Now normally, Philmore kept his distance from that side of the family—on account of the scandal between The Captain and Allan's daughter, Fanny Brier—but we listened with hushed amazement as Dean read the will of Phil's father and our minds buried themselves in wonder. I was no lawyer, but it seemed to spell out that the ownership of the Laithe property would pass to Philmore upon the death of The Captain's last blood relative and tenant of the estate—none other than that same Allan Laithe.

I felt relieved at once, even with my dad's health on the brink of failure, and felt such bolstered devotion to my husband as I pondered moving back to Phelps County to live on the land that was rightfully Philmore's to inherit. But I was still by my father's bedside, turning fear and worry over in my hands, and praying he could only make it to Jefferson City. The stroke had been a terrible fright to me, and understanding that I was flustered over the phone, Philmore offered to drive up to St. Louis and get me. He told me to leave my car in the city while he came in his truck to take me home.

"Hold on, Jackie," he said, after I urged him to stay in Eminence for the night and get me the next morning. "Here's my plan," he went on, "I'm gonna take a nice drive on a beautiful night and meet you on the floor that takes you across the bridge to the hotel. Then we'll have a nice stroll to the Euclid garage."

Moments such as that often went unappreciated in their time because of the illusion of urgency; for we fear the unknown. But it has always humbled me how at once the tapestry of worry can dissolve when a memory is recalled later on, and the moments left to take on the nostalgia of the past with them—as they did that night when I listened from the dark corner of the estate to the wind howling down the stone chimney.

Already I was back to the eve of my second husband's death. And since at times English fails to explain the true nature of something, or gets tongue-tied with false meaning, let me not misconstrue it by saying that it was the second husband of mine *who* died—but rather, that it was the second husband of mine *to* die. Luckily, I had become so acquainted with grief that I barely flinched at the second. If anything, I viewed it as the proper evil to complete (or perhaps to progress by one-third) that which had already begun to unfold at the death of the first.

I heard the molten glass scalding as Benton held the rod in the furnace before a final temperament, vainly relating the solemnity with which he performed his trade to my burden of irrevocable loss. I felt miserable with the grief that I had neither one of the men who had both constituted the whole of my life. Philmore and my father were gone, and it was not simply that the burden existed, but rather that it could not also be tempered and cooled like the hot glass. Even the outlet of my writing left me, which had regularly proven to be my escape. For now I could not even steal a glance at my typewriter without feeling sorrow, or even the small lamp on my desk which I had always relished the joy in turning off after a long night of working.

It was never the same after Phil left; for ultimately it was he who saw the light in my words, and gave me the courage to shine that light as well. He would tell me, after coming home from the mines with that grit-like quality of smoke still in his lungs:

"Made a fine sunset tonight driving home to you, Jackie. Thought to myself, 'if I's a writer, I could capture it. Maybe my wife could'."

My heart leapt for him a measurable degree, as anyone who has been in love may come to understand. It was as if he had said, from behind the sound of his own words:

"Jackie, why don't you put on this little lamp? There. Now take out some blank sheets of paper. Look at them for a while, sweet, and see if you can't find what stories are hidden in them."

It was something about his voice, perhaps. The way he dispensed profound thoughts in short words that sounded like home, disguising themselves as mere rambles from the mind of a simple boy. Though he led a dark life in the mines, choking on the coal-black dust and smoke, the promises of love he felt for me were lodged in each word.

I yearned for the moments he tipped the scale of our sour-sweet, undefined and indispensable love toward me—starting in the shallow cleft at the bottom of my neck. It was a place meant for him; he found it with his lips against my throat and then the darkness and coal tunnels went away from him. All was bright, and pink, and there was a redeeming tunnel of light. An endless tunnel which came out from below, from me, which Philmore rose up into. There was no fear of caving in on him or his men, nor a wish of escaping. Perhaps he even wanted to feel as if he could make a home there—a home in my love. We thought of surrender and made a treatise instead, coming together to make love and be each other's retreat in the years of passion; but it was not long before the smoke shriveled his lungs and the very land to which he gave his workingman's heart and soul, finally reclaimed the same for its own.

I lived in that place in my mind for as long as I could get away with, until the sounds of glasswork ceased outside. Benton had come inside and now filled the doorway with his bulky frame. His intrusion was even less predictable than his brother Jed's had been, but I did not feel the same anger I had against the latter. *How could I hold anything against Ben?* I couldn't—not even the noises that echoed throughout the walls of the house. For my mind had mechanically substituted the symphony of Benton's final shaping of the glass with that of the wind pushing against the timbers of the estate. It was an ocean of sound for the vacuum of my mind; and now Benton stood there, staring into me, or through me, and held something out.

I had turned to look at him, for he was far larger than Jed and able to block out more of the light, and with horror I saw what he was holding out to me. I dreaded the threat that this item revealed, the effect that his workmanship would inevitably produce; so I scorned him with everything in me. I felt a wrath that came from within, and with one swift arc I knocked the bulb out of his hands. I was attacked with a piercing pain in my head, a pressure that had somehow not been provoked by his constant pounding, but instead rose sharply as the shards of the bulb spilled out in all directions against the floor. The hollow nook of sound that was left in the air after the glass shattered was filled by a horrible moan. It was a low, groaning cry that Benton let out while picking up the pieces into his hands.

I felt not a shred of the remorse I should have felt. The grief I had bequeathed to Benton simply gave more direction and clarity to it. The light began to fade around me as it did with migraines of similar strength. I suddenly heard the phrase repeated to me by the lawyer, earlier that afternoon, which I did not understand in the least. It was deafening.

"Brier, Barren, Bloodroot," he had said.

I only recognized the flowers. They were in my garden earlier that year, picked in the spring, preserved through the summer, and enjoyed in the lonely months. I cherished to save the flowers of the bloodroot from being choked by the wind, knighting them survivors by twisting their stems and hanging them in the nursery. But right then, reliving the ambiguity of Dean's phrase only throbbed my temples more, so I turned my thoughts away from it.

Benton was gone, and I was able to pick up where I left off—thinking of my truest love as a feeble but dignified attempt at maintaining the shreds of my sanity. It felt like my own mind had shattered into pieces on the floor instead of the lightbulb Benton made me. And I saw Philmore again.

It was during the final hours, when he was nearly suffocated by his own coal-black lungs. Phil told me he wanted the treatment to stop, that he wanted to savor whatever time he had left with me. I prayed that night, putting my hands on his arm and feeling how ice-cold his skin was. It was late into the night, the interval where all semblance of time goes away and clocks tell nothing, and I felt a warm hand move into mine. I couldn't believe the change I felt; not in his breathing, for he still wheezed and drew hollow breath into his lungs, but that his hand was burning. I prayed, thanking God, until we both drifted away—me to sleep, he to somewhere else.

Benton

You have a wife.

The furnace gave me spit and it hurt my hand but I got more of the Shine made; there was too much darkness in her room so I told Jackie I'd make her one. *She was my wife.* I made the crucible go by puttin' the fire back on. With the punty rod I could make all darkness go away. The lightbulb would shine like the sun for my wife—I would work through the night to finish it. Couldn't sleep anyways cause anytime I started to drift I woke to the ambush that *wasn't* there and the flashes ringin' out around me. But it was almost worse to wake up to the quiet that *was* there. I didn't understand it. That was war and this was my pain and all I wished was to have a nice anvil to lay my head on and someone to smash my head in 'gainst the crucible—but *Tom said that was a rotten way of sayin' it.* Tom was the one I talked to about war and about losing Fanny and Phil and even Benton. *Me, I mean.* Benton was me and Tom said not to separate the two. I was workin' on that.

I shared about the chopper going down and the major cryin' on the walkie. That was right before I deserted. My pack was wet through and the M16 jammed as soon as I pulled the action back to lock it in place. Two men fell down and died in my foxhole after they tried runnin' towards the LMG. Was like they lost all their bones as soon as they got hit. They went limp and fell into my ditch.

I grabbed the blowpipe and moved to dip it in the glory hole, right before putting it in the lehr—the last step in makin' Jackie a Shine. Tom said it was good to talk about these things. Tom asked about the choppers circling above my head and I told him I had a wife and he asked more about when Christ's second coming failed. I told him about my wedding and he said I didn't really have a wife; that it wasn't good to make things up. He asked me about the room with the wallpaper and I told him about the Shine. I would put the Shine in Jackie's room for her to see through the darkness— *she was my wife.*

"Benton," Tom said. "Do you remember the breathing I showed you? Place a hand on your lower stomach right here and try to fill your lungs from your diaphragm. Yes, Benton. Yes. That's it."

"Fanny is dead and Philmore is too and I miss them. But Jedediah is still 'round. I am Benton because it is better to be *me* than anyone else. You said so Tom."

"I am glad you aren't separating yourself from your experiences, Ben. It shows great progress. Are you ready to *brief* me on your week?"

I heard the word and it stood out among the others.

*　　　　*　　　　*

"Brief us, Private," Lieutenant Marsh said. "How many in your company were killed?"

"All the men are dead. I am not dead…can't hear 'cause the grenades." Then:

"Ran here fast as I could; have no company left. They's all dead, Sir. Enemy stomped us. Ambushed in the night."

"Private Brier, are you fit to give a full report?" Lieutenant Marsh said.

"Yes, Sir. I ran away from my company during the fighting and followed a stream until I made it home. I wanna go home. There is a room with flowers on the wallpaper."

Lieutenant Marsh breathed in and shouted to Corporal Lewis outside. "Get the Private to the medical tent, Corporal," he said. "Tell Doc I want a full physical and mental evaluation."

"Yes, Lieutenant," the corporal said.

But I had an idea—

"Lieutenant, sir." I said. "I dirtied my pants and slept in them while my company was killed. I want to leave. Will Doc send me home?"

It was all I could do not to break down in the medical tent. Head poundin'. I told Doc it was like the feeling of a metal rod anglin' down against my head; like the marver smoothin' and crushin' my head against hot iron.

"Why should I send you home and not the other wounded men in this unit?" the Doc said. "Answer me, Private."

"Doc…" I said.

I made my thoughts straight and knew there was some way to make them come out true—just like Phil did so many times, tellin' me smart phrases and asking me to repeat them to him. He said good words would get me out of a jam if I ever got in one.

"I live off a green place by the Phelps County line in Miss'ura next to a big piece o' land," I said it true as could be. It was just how Phil told me. His words and way of talking came out. "I want to go home, Sir."

"So do the others in here, Private. You see?"

"But I need to go home to that green piece," I said. "My company's all dead, and there's sun shining on the backs o' the cattle at home. And I have shit in my pants. Sir."

"Private," said the Doc. "I'll send you home if you give Corporal Lewis a full report."

*   *   *

I went home a week after that and found the other war at home across from Mama's grave; a war in the graveyard, the soldiers with rifles closing in on the western front. I told Tom the whole story. It went this way:

"After the flashes and the grenades and the enemy's God coming down and touchin' the earth and sprayin' the ground with bullets, I played dead and made it home. And I'm not talkin' about the first war no more. The second war I went to was when Mama died and 21 gunshots sounded out all around me. I had no company then and there was no objective and Mama was dead all a'sudden when the hole was closed over her. It was nothing but dark, so dark. And that's all I'll say about it."

"Breathe, Benton," Tom said. "Breathe."

That was earlier today. Now it was just me and the crucible. Just me and my thoughts and having a wife. It was dark all around me and the wind came up rustlin' the trees. I got spooked. I thought of my company and how it must'a been their dead voices howlin' from the trees and hauntin' me. I prayed to the God of Abr'am and Isaac and Jacob then—like Reverend Milton told me—praying He'd let me finish the Shine for Jackie. *It was near done.*

I worked at it and it was all done. Just needed the filaments now. I thought not-war thoughts like Tom told me to do when I got spooked. Like when I was littler with Dad by the stream and trout jumping out of the water. Jed and Phil and I fishin'. Dad there; okay with me being with him and my brothers 'cause no one was there to call me a Bastard or Cousin-Trash or Retard. Stepping in the big mud prints Dad left behind. I had to jump-hop-skip into them along the stream and Jed behind me pointin' back behind us; he seen a trout. He was older'n me and I thought he was right so I casted my line hard and looked up. It was caught in the tree.

"HA, HA," Jed roared out. His shoulders up down up down—stomach shakin' laughin'. Phil helped me get my line untangled. I missed Phil but I knew he must'a left us for a reason.

I was done with the Shine besides the filaments now. They'd make it glow. But you could still look at it and it was like lookin' into a round globe. My face was in the glass bulb lookin' at me and I got scared by the wind again. My dead company whispering to me.

Tom was far away but Jackie was second best. Could talk to your wife and feel put together and almost whole again. Inside the house I walked around until I was outside Jackie's room. Light coming in from the hall and the sight of my wife sleepin'.

"Jackl'in, made a Shine for you," I said. "Well...maybe have it done for you by next week with the filaments in."

I showed her the glass in my hand. Stretched it out toward her. "This says Jackie is your wife," I said, like Phil would'a said it just then. Phil always talked nice to Jackie so I figured I would; but what I said must'a not been good. Wife turned her face at me.

The enemy reached for my M16 but there was only a bulb in my hands. It scared me and I seen the enemy with his bayonet and I wasn't quick enough to stop him from getting the Shine outta my hands. There was a gun or grenade that went off in the room and I didn't know where or how or when Doc would send me home till I opened my eyes and saw Jackie and the wallpaper again. I looked down at where the grenade went off and saw glass all over the floor. Water from my eyes was coming down, coating my hands. Dropped to the floor. Picking the shards of glass up with my hands so blood was covering me just like in the foxholes and I moaned and moaned and cried and wanted to die. I couldn't talk to my wife and couldn't force myself to clean it all up. Remembered the medic saying something to me about death.

"Death cleans up better'n bandages," he said with his face snarled up like he was angry.

The medic was all I could think of. Ran out of the room and into the livin' room and knew I could clean the blood off my hands. War was blood and bandages and shards of glass in your soul. Jackie was your wife. *Is your wife.* Benton is me. *I am.* Tom couldn't help me now, but there was something I could do.

The flower book on the table made me younger again; daddy showing us the pictures—pointing to each one. I flipped away from 'Brier' and found the one I always liked: the ones Mama planted at the side of the house.

Breathe like Tom said. But I couldn't breathe. I was doing the up-down shoulder laugh but nothin' funny and no air coming in and I was out of breath. I was scared and heard the flashes and the grenades comin' again and my dead company howlin' from the trees outside. Jackie didn't want the Shine or me. I still needed to clean up the mess. I looked up at the fan on the ceilin' and saw it spinnin'—helicopter blades beatin' the air—and I ran out of the living room, ducking the shots. I flipped the switch that turned the choppers off and sent them away and I saw that I could reach one of the blades. I brought a chair in from the kitchen table right underneath. The medic was talking to me in my head.

"Death cleans up better'n bandages."

Harmony

The movies always romanticized trauma. It was all still a long way off, though. I hadn't even woken up yet; and even if I had just then, it would still have taken me years to acknowledge the grief.

Adelaide had already done the dying an hour before I woke. It was like I said. No theatrics. There may have been some spit on the side of her mouth, some sick on her shirt showing she had choked on it, but otherwise she looked just how a sleeping person looked. Her head was back. There was morning light coming in from the window so that I could see her neck tilted, mouth open. I felt nauseous from how stuffy the van was. I opened the door in a panic.

The air we had started with in the night had been good, because it was shared and exchanged; love was made with it. The air it turned into was bad air, the kind that stopped circulating through two pairs of lungs and had to be filtered through one. Whatever kind she had breathed out at the very end came through mine, so I imagine I breathed in the last of Addie's life—though I could not have thought of it that way in the moment. I only saw that there was a body and it reminded me of my birth mom's old dog that laid down behind the sage bushes one morning. His eyes were glassy with that long-gone look when we found him.

I gasped for the breeze coming from the river valley below. It got rid of most of the head haze. There was no sound from the top of the hill where the estate sat. I got sick outside the van and went over to the body. I put my mouth on hers and compressed her chest. She was in a stiff position with the curve of the neck back, one of her hands under the guitar.

The hills of Newburg were filled with a dissonance that needed a remedy. The mold of my life was laid out before me, and I felt purpose in being poured over it once more. When I thought of others, it didn't make sense to me. The fact that Jedediah would come right back down the hill in his truck in a few hours, driving out to the farm like any other day, was a strange idea. It was as if the night had no bearing on the events of the morning.

I then heard a shouting uncommon to Jedediah or anyone that lived in the estate up the hill. It was close to Benton when he was having one of his episodes, but this was not a sound Benton made. It *was* Uncle Jed!

A horrible worry seized me, forcing the deferred anguish over Addie to take hold of my heart. I half-crawled, half-ran up the hill. Jedediah's name never fully escaped my throat, but I found him eventually. We knelt together in the living room where our insufferable nights converged into one shared grief.

Jedediah

Lots o' folks didn't think there was substance in nostalgia. That familiar smell on the wind from a different season and time. They's mistaken. In fact, one o' those was on the air right then, waftin' through the window and waking me up. It smelled like a night wind stirring up bass in a pond, like playin' a game of sardines with Phil out in the field and even Ben too when dad let him play with us.

Forbiddin' us to mess around with Benton was the Cap'n's way of savin' face. Didn't want no one to know that boy was really a Laithe through and through. But for all the secrecy, and the lack of practice Ben had with us, he sure was one of the best sardines players you'd ever seen. We'd go over to Fanny's and ask him to play 'cause it was boring without him. He got so good at it, he started changin' his hiding spot on us in the middle of a game—even getting one of us to see him on purpose so's we could hide with him and give him a challenge. He was a natural.

That was the smell—the same smell—rising on the night breeze. It was the aroma of hide and seek in the pastures and comin' home with burrs all over our clothes, of smellin' roast in the pot and telling Benton to stay for supper.

I felt the mornin' light hit my face hard now; it was late morning's light the way it slanted across me—I'd never slept in so late in my life. *What was it about that room that made me sleep so long?* I rubbed my face with my hands, thinkin' about that chicken trailer I needed to get moved by the end o' the day—*those laying hens were gonna get goin' any day now.* I was out of bed and went to see what the raucous was all about last night. I knew it was poor Ben's glass that shattered all over the floor.

And there it was, shards trailin' out o' the door where Jacqueline was still sleeping. I saw her easy now with the light from the rest o' the house fillin' the hallway. That was one thing about that house, the way it filled with brightness. The natural light came in from the back where I looked at the range and didn't see Benton anywhere near it. *God help us*, I thought. Any day that man-child didn't start at the crucible would be a day o' reck'nin'. A day to keep a close eye on the ol' boy so's he wouldn't hurt himself or have another episode. Sure as anything, that crucible did more for the family than even Benton realized. No matter why he did it, the range was exorcisin' his demons. I looked back in the room at Jackie and saw her sleeping how she slept from time to time—mouth open and head back, breathin' steady.

I knew I had a life bond with her. Jackie sure tore up all my insides at times, but she meant a different thing in her eyes—I believed that. And when she woke, I'd be there to care for her. Benton didn't know how but that wasn't against him. I went in and looked down at her, came close and held one strand o' hair that came free. I moved it behind her ear and whispered somethin' in there for only me and her, quiet and true. It took me a minute to clean up the glass on the floor, but I used the pan in the hallway and made sure it was safe for her to walk when she got up.

But it wouldn't matter none too much that she was comfortable after I went in the livin' room. My hollerin' woke her up. Soon as I yelled and rushed over to that thing hangin' from the ceiling fan, the day o' reck'nin' showed itself.

Folks like Benton had no place in this world, so they always found their way out of it. I was on the floor holdin' his body like I'd done years before at his mama's funeral, except he was the not-alive one now. I felt all small-faced and stupid, cryin' again like that. Of all the hidin' places he found when we were kids, over all the pastures and in all the forests, I never 'spected he'd hide in so clumsy a place as that. It was in plain sight. Maybe that's why the ol' boy was so good at sardines—he knew when to make himself seen and when not to. And Jackie didn't do so much as make a whimper for her own husband dead and gone.

She came in from my hollerin', sat down on the sofa, and pulled the rug over Benton's face after I got him down. Harmony came in the back door. She told us what happened to Adelaide. There was a talk about graves. I said I'd figured out Benton's a long time ago, so we didn't have to worry over it. *And that was true.* I found it the day I shot the dying bitch by the stream and saw a shaded area close by.

110

Reverend Milton

The crowd was growing. The old and the young of Newburg. Folks from Jeff City. Relatives from Hannibal. Family from St. Louis and Kansas City. Mourners crawled out of every corner of Miss'ura that day. Even newborns were present. They were carried in by the soon-deads and those in the middle of the two ages, and presiding over everyone was the sobriety to congregate in such a spirit as remembrance.

Military men were adorned in their full uniforms with berets on the sides of their heads. The Laithes were present and the Briers came also; it was a day for remembering a death because the life behind it had already been forgotten. I had a verse for my sermon, and it was swell because they were sacred words. It was Hebrews 12:1-2 in King James Version:

> *Wherefore seeing we also are compassed about with so great a cloud of witnesses, let us lay aside every weight, and the sin which doth so easily beset us, and let us run with patience the race that is set before us, looking unto Jesus the author and finisher of our faith; who for the joy that was set before him endured the cross, despising the shame, and is set down at the right hand of the throne of God.*

It was written well and I knew it was, so I best not add too much of my own words around it. Poetry cleaned up poorly. It was not meant to be polished, and Scripture would not offend anyone by being left bare. I knew that all I had to do, to save any souls that may still be lost on that day (for it was my calling to reach those who had not yet been reached), was to say the least I could possibly get away with.

But against all proper notions, I remembered a lousy thing. And lousy it was, in this context, to recall Dean saying to me before the first memorial service I ever officiated:

"Yes, Reverend. A shame to hear about Mrs. Levitt. She was on hospice, yes? Then at the very least it was not a surprise. I may sound cynical, but it keeps me paid—there's business in this rotten stuff." He said.

I suppose his sentiment offered practicality for him, but it also struck too true a chord in my profession to be taken lightly. For indeed, the noble work of evangelism was best done around the solemnity of the grave. Furthermore, adjacency to death could not be expressed as urgently as at a funeral, for the most powerful factor in communicating the presence of death to those who are not sick or dying themselves was to see the dead, to stand near, to touch. Alas, anyone who feared religion neighboring death was a fool; for an acknowledgement of mortality was the soil on which the seeds of faith could be sown.

Nevertheless, there was a tightness in my chest from the weight of my calling upon me. I looked across the center aisle at the members of the Gaffer's Guild who took up the second row—directly behind the family. Every man and woman who had worked with Benton, and trained him, and inevitably learned from him in his craft at the crucible, was present to pay their respects for his legacy. It was something magnanimous in his life; I would have to say at least one thing about that. *I must not forget.*

Before I rose from my seat and approached the pulpit, I looked upon those faces in the crowd, bereaved and without relief. I felt the sun at length fall upon the graveyard for the first time that afternoon; and it was as if I had lost my import. With the light slanting into the eyes and faces of the crowd, my message and words were blotted out by the magnitude of the heat hanging in the late summer day.

But I did not let this trouble my heart. I even rationalized the whole service to myself when I left the stand, finding a silent place to collect my own reasoning for the tragic and untimely death of Benton Brier in the night earlier that week. I rationalized that, at most, all I could do—and any man of God could ever do in times of loss—was to dress death in the burial linens of grace, to anoint the heads of mourners with the sweet perfume of Scripture, and to point them back to the mercy of God. It was a foolish endeavor to think that grieving was made any less retched from the ceremony, but even Benton himself looked happier from behind the embalming agents and makeup than he ever did living, and that's what disturbed me. *The chemicals preserved his body, but who would care for his spirit?*

I felt particularly concerned with the wellness of the bereaved family, for I had carried a close correspondence with the Briers and the Laithes for all of Benton's life. Furthermore, despite the words I said about him which were all but forgotten, the service did a lousy job of explaining his untimely suicide. And without laying out the whys and wherefores to folks, all the rest of this felt like just a playact.

I remembered nearly every second after Jedediah called me that afternoon. In fact, I learned very quickly that he had asked for me before he even dialed the hospital. I came promptly to the estate, parking my car without care or concern for the landscaping alongside the drive, for I knew it was dire. The front right tire had veered into the path, nudging a small bush into a square plot of soil where the bloodroot bloomed only months before, just like it had every April since the long-dead Captain decreed it with his own fastidious zeal in the name of tradition.

At this time of year, the garden had been excavated. The flowers that went unpicked had passed away, and the dirt was dry from the cool wind coming from the valley. I walked up the wooden steps that merged with the long porch and opened the door to the harrowing scene. The stiff body under the rug and the rope tied to the ceiling trusses did not let my imagination wander far. I was astounded at the lack of commotion among the three gathered in the living room.

"Jed, I came as quick as I could," I said. "But son, why did you not call an ambulance?"

"What for? Already picked a grave for him," Jedediah said. "There's a few spades out in the lean-to on the property. I just wanted you to bless 'im. Could you—could you say a prayer for ol' Ben, Reverend?"

How were we to know he couldn't be resuscitated? It must have been the sound of Jed's voice, or that quality in it that pulled at me, which stopped me from calling someone right then. I went to the quiet group beside the rug and knelt next to Benton, placed one hand over him, and prayed.

Harmony looked touched by something from the way she was looking on. I felt the occasion warranted more than met the eye. I asked her if she had been the one to find Benton, but she shook her head. I started the painstaking process of comforting them—telling Jed that he should stay put for a minute while I called an ambulance. It took some convincing.

"Benton was a man who many people cared for; it wouldn't be right to bury him in the field like a dog." I said.

I didn't get much outright support for my idea of calling an ambulance, but in one reply I was given both Jed's acquiescence and Harmony's missing piece to the story.

"You'll have to call two cars," he said.

*   *   *

After I stepped back from the van and saw the last of the bodies off, the ambulances transporting the presumed dead and both Harmony and Jacqueline to see after them, I was deeply shaken. Adelaide left less questions behind than Benton, but there was still the feeling of their shared absence. They had created a vacuum you could step into and feel.

I went back up the drive to survey the scene, found the living room empty, and after a moment I nearly believed I had lost all my wits. I made out the familiar ringing of a rod against metal rails in the backyard—where the sound had always come from—as if nothing had changed and I would see Benton back at the range like always. I peered out the back door and saw that it was Jedediah, dismantling the furnace and all of its components before the treads of the ambulances had even disappeared from the ground. I was troubled, but I knew each man had a different way of handling grief. That was another thing I learned at funerals.

I said a prayer for myself then, asking God to reveal something to me so I could make sense of it all. Whether it be divine Providence or coincidence, I knew what I was asking for; and it was answered. As I passed back through the house and surveyed each room, I saw an open book on the coffee table in the living room, right under the ceiling fan where Benton was found. The book was one of many items I had developed a fondness toward, since I had been relatively on-call as a minister for the Laithes over the years. "Missouri

Landscapes and Wildflowers" was its name—opened to a particular species:

The bloodroot is a plant native to Missouri, whose flowers have a bright orange sap that is poisonous. The flowers bloom before the leaves come out, leaving the flowers to appear unprotected on the stalks.

That flower was one of The Captain's favorites. Even Dean Elliot mentioned it in the paper that very morning. How strange these things were! But not coincidence. The meaning of the phrase was coming into view now.

Brier. Barren. Bloodroot. I knew it was the will of Providence granting me clairvoyance so I could carry out the message from the book, and, translating God's voice into human reasoning—that a Brier had died, leaving a barren widow behind, and the enduring symbolism of redemption for the lineage: *Jedediah.* For he had bloomed before the leaves came out, and the estate left unprotected on the stalks.

I would tell Dean first thing.

November 18, 1979

Bloodroot. A poison which was not the pride but the curse of the land. And there came the discussion.

The reputable and shamed, the chosen and unchosen. No one drew the line. Not yet. But there was a draught that could kill both men if they drank from the same cup. An elixir indifferent to reputation or even destitution.

It was in the name—the appraiser of bloodlines, examiner of the root of evil. But was it the sole harbinger of fate? The poison was, yes, strong enough to kill either man. So who would master it, the Bloodroot, and could it tip the scales?

Dean Elliot

There are intermissions when it serves to have a refreshment. A cold drink of remembrance to coat the entourage of consecutive nows. It seems in good fashion therefore, at this time, to serve the wine, to slaughter the fattened calf; to bid the guests to take off their shoes and recall that which they have heard up to this point. As a journalist, nonetheless, it would be remiss of me not to indulge him or her presently. Let us start with the place and time.

In those days, Newburg in Central Missouri was the stain on the rug of the union; Phelps County, in which it lay, the snagged fabric on the nation's garments. The people in the town of Newburg were a heart-hardened people who were only ever gathering or departing from each other.

Descending from the bloodlines of the gypsies, the once-nomadic people of Newburg fell into their old ways. Soon, the townsfolk were always busying or idling themselves (hardly a far cry from their fabled past), and found that the only means by which a man could offer fellowship to his neighbor was through rescinding his own dread solitude. This was meager but admirable for the people of the town, who, despite their habitual practices, could not be easily roused or excited—yet neither were their spirits ever truly broken. That society, and that place, made a man grow to love and miss and forget it, just so that he may remember it all over again. It could be said to be a journeyman's town. For in those years, Newburg was neither here nor there. It just was.

And it may also entertain the historians looking upon these manuscripts, squinting their eyes together and scrupulously discussing what could have caused such an unimportant but inevitably disillusioned community to lay itself threadbare on the flames of destruction; indeed, it may entertain him or her to hear an account of the scribe's own enlightenment, or rather his descent into the fields of unenviable and irrevocable knowledge.

It started with an itch, of course, and as most things did, eventually culminated to a nuisance I had no choice but to scratch at. The discomfort grew stronger if I paused after starting, so I found it unavoidable to be wholly engrossed with the pursuit of information, and to seek it out even when my own mental fortitude was in question. I was slowly unlatching locked parts of the story. And that was all it took for me to discern that I was ever nearer to uncovering a secret in the family's reputation—the blind spot in their armor, if the Laithes had even been equipped with such defenses at all.

I met with the reverend and decided to keep my suspicions from him until he revealed his. If I could emerge without drawing first, mine would be the smoking gun. For I believed Milton knew something I didn't, and if I could unsheathe it from him, I would pitch it against the information I had gathered over the last few months—information I was able to unearth during a visit to the Laithe estate. But I would conceal that piece until I needed it.

"The book was the part that made me feel strange," Milton said. "All those years The Captain curated a garden in his front yard with bright flowers—the one kind, with white blossoms and orange-red roots—and Jacqueline planting it all over again." He shook his head, and unclasped his hands, then continued.

"The Captain said the bloodroot and its properties revealed something about the chaos in all of us, and there the flower showed up again—even after disappearing from the garden and adorning Jed's childhood room—in the open book beneath the very place Benton's body was found." The reverend finished with his mouth askew, in a kind of grimace.

I thought I saw him get startled, or have a twitch of the spine, but made no comment on it and allowed the visual that Milton shared—the link between the symbol and the suicide—to take effect. I convinced myself to practice restraint out of respect for the dead and relented my questioning; but soon I couldn't resist.

"And what of it, Reverend?" I said. "The book. It's hardly something to feel ominous about, unless you believe in ghosts or something of that nature. Not the Holy Ghost, I mean." I corrected myself.

Milton thought this possibility uninspired, most likely due to his religion, for he leaned his elbows onto his desk and said:

"You saw them, didn't you? It was the time of year that also bothered me. Late summer, far past when any bloodroot should have been in bloom; and it was none other than that very white flower in Jed's room, suspended from the ceiling by the stem; the same flower that could be found shooting up through the nursery hatches of the garden in early spring. Jacqueline was keeping them for a reason, but I never got the impression that she was incredibly sentimental about Benton's passing."

"You're talking about gardening. I want to talk about matters of importance, now, Reverend. That's why I came, since we have both known the Laithe family longer than anyone in this town."

"Isn't that what I am getting at?" Milton said. "The most curious thing to me was the change in behavior of Jacqueline after her second husband passed.

"How do you mean?" I said.

"Have you not visited and seen for yourself; the way the widow was given a jolt of energy all of a sudden, remembering to tend to the flowers again, picking and preserving them, becoming involved in taking care of the estate, even looking after Harmony as well as she has been?" he said. "That girl may be Philmore's blood, but Jackie didn't do a lick for her before."

I wanted to say something, but wasn't fast enough.

"You also were touched mysteriously by the words—I saw it!" Milton said, his eyes widening. "The signs and pictures from the book, the one The Captain paraded around with. He would show them to anyone who walked the grounds."

"Why—"

"You said it in your interview, Dean," the reverend said. "The morning paper, the day you retired—*Brier, Barren, Bloodroot.* You know there must be significance in it."

"I don't get it," I said.

"Have you become so disillusioned, so confiscated of all soundness of mind and shield of logic and reasoning, to not see the credible threat any longer?" Milton said.

"You speak in riddles," I said. "I don't understand." But this time I didn't let him start again.

"Let me tell you what I saw when I visited the Laithe estate," I continued. "It was only last week, and you will be happy to hear about the flowers; they were moved to a new room. It might reveal Jackie's intention behind them."

Reverend Milton indicated that he was interested about what I had seen, and despite my reluctance to abet time in diminishing the story's dignity, I waited for him as he rose from his desk, walked to the door behind me, shut it, and returned to his seat. He quickly said a prayer to himself. After the prayer, he lighted the candle on his desk and said,

"Yes. Let me hear what it was, with the audience of the Lord and the saints our witnesses."

This melodramatic prompting of my story was something that any journalist seldom favored, as they—or in this case, I—preferred that the import of the story not be biased from the occasion of its telling. Nevertheless, I began. And for effect, let it be paraphrased with a duplicity of connotation that at the time I did not comprehend, but which now demanded an all-new translation:

"The house, hallowed and unbright, stood as always at the top of the drive. I parked at the bottom of the hill so as not to disrupt the tranquility present, which I believed to be precious to those who were mourning. I had already told Jacqueline I intended to check on Jedediah, that I may see that he was taken care of and given rightful possession of his late father's assets. I was almost at the top now.

"The cold wind made the stone buttresses of the estate seem more chiseled. I looked along the path that diverted around the house toward the backyard, and saw the earth of the garden hardened and bare. I knocked on the door and, before it was opened, tried to remember an image of the untilled lines in Jedediah's earth-bound smile—the kind of simple expression that came from living on pastures scored with hoof marks and manure. I caught a small moment of recollection, then quickly unremembered all at the sight I beheld as Jacqueline opened the door for me." I said to the reverend before briefly pausing, and commenced again in haste.

"It was a still-life in progress, if it could be compared to a painting. The cold light crept in through the blinds, hardly justifying the empty expressions of those in the house. I stood in the foyer which connected to the living room on the left. The living room appeared imbued with dead memories and memories of the dead. The ceiling trusses, the ominous members that suggested death; the coffee table, once laden with reference books for The Captain's lost prophecies, but holding none on it any longer; and the dining room on the right, where two strangers sat at the table. Jacqueline walked through the adjoining room from the kitchen to greet me. Our exchange was short, abridged with the magnitude of uncertainty that hung in the room. I asked her how things had been since the funeral, and if the new lawyer was taking care of the family. Jacqueline said she was meeting with him regularly on Jedediah's behalf, and I was taken aback at this—that Jed himself would not have wanted to handle his own family's affairs.

"Of course, by now my attention was drawn to one of the strangers at the dinner table. There was a grown man with all-white eyes. I offered my hand to him, asking who I had the pleasure of meeting, but as his face turned, I was filled with an uneasiness. It was a face I had known all too well despite the absence of familiarity in his milky eyes which looked straight through me. 'Why, Dean, you know who this is,' Jacqueline said. 'This is Jedediah. My husband.'

"I will break from the story and the horror embodied by that title alone—this apparent husbandry through which the Laithe estate had yet again been ushered into the hands of the widow—and request evidence from you and the power vested in you, Reverend, to please validate or invalidate what cannot be a rightful covenant. For although she introduced him as such, there was no certificate of marriage."

The reverend stood up again and walked over to his bookcase, where he kept many of his documents, licenses, and holy papers. He handed me a portfolio which showed a certificate in bold print, triggering the recall of a long-unremembered moment—the day I had held the marriage certificate of Benton and Jacqueline.

"But they had not filed for it, Reverend. There is not enough to validate their union, is there? I am a man studied in law—enough to know the regulations from the state on such a topic. The sharpness of my intellect has not run dry. Their marriage cannot be established!"

"It is, Dean," the reverend said. "It was I who married them."

That was the blow. It was not a shot I saw coming but one that tore through the flesh before the sound of the bullet ever reached me.

"I didn't know," I said, then tried something else.

"Answer me this—is Jedediah still eligible for the inheritance mentioned in the will of his father's, when it clearly states that the owner of the birthright must have lived on the estate for up to 7 years prior? Jedediah lived on the farm; it's not possible."

"You forget, Dean, that for many years Jedediah was able to have dual residency—as a tenant of the land at the farm and a resident of the Laithe estate," the reverend said. "In fact, he would have had such a status for the entire duration of 7 years—the time between Philmore and Jacqueline moving in during the summer of '72 and Benton's passing. I will remind you, it was Benton's to inherit before Jedediah by the same 7-year rule; for after he was discharged from the military in '71, Benton had moved in with Allan Laithe and remained its only tenant after Allan passed. That is, until you called Phil to tell him he had just become eligible to usurp the birthright upon returning home."

There was a hushed eloquence in his voice, as if an alloy of two kinds of authority had been forged from his proclamation. The reverend had made his second draw, smelting an ingot of terseness from the fire.

"I cannot accept this," I said.

"Life affords no man privilege to deny what the Lord has made plain," he said.

"There's more at stake here, you know, Milton. Surely you can reverse that which has been established on the grounds of a moral ambiguity. Why, your very religion suggests that none should be living under the same roof together without a holy union under God. And here was Jedediah, for years after Jacqueline was widowed, taking care of her as if they were already wedded!"

He opened his Bible, which had been underneath his hand as I had spoken, and turned to a passage before granting me his reply.

"Marriage is honourable in all, and the bed undefiled: but whoremongers and adulterers God will judge. Hebrews 13:4," he said. "I am not to serve as an accuser, for my sins are not less than those of Jedediah, or Jacqueline—"

"Close the book," I said. "I get it; I shouldn't have said anything."

Milton was startled but not offended; he had doubtless seen worse rejections of Scripture. "Dean, I consider you a friend," he said. "To assure us both, I will send my own wife to the estate this morning. She will tell me how they are getting on—she's good with lost sheep. This was last week, you say? Tell me what else you saw; ease my pain about Jed's condition."

I was reluctant, but resumed the rest of my story. I was starting to relax my body finally, which had become rigid and taut from the blood curdling at the thought of such a union sanctified in the eyes of the State—one that could bring the ultimate downfall to the Laithes which 7 years before I had sworn to prevent.

"I learned from Jacqueline," I said, "that the fateful suicide of Benton had given Jedediah emotional anguish and worsened his cataracts, taking away his eyesight. The doctor called it hysterical blindness."

"And what of the other stranger?" the reverend asked.

"It was a helpless, loveless, small child. The greatest failure of the family. She was finally under the roof now and out of the cold biting wind, which the van that once sheltered her was useless to protect her from. You can guess from this description, that it was Harmony. But it was not the same body that she had once occupied; for there was a limpness in her that showed her veins and bones ripping at her flesh to come out. She looked in bad health—almost deathly. I could only imagine this was on account of losing her intimate partner and uncle in the same night, from vastly different but equally horrendous causes. She did not eat anymore; this was apparent. It became clear to me that the role Jacqueline now held—nourishing both a decrepit girl and a grown man emaciated with lamentations—thereby empowered her to assume the role of proprietor and caretaker of the property." I said, clearing my throat before starting again.

"I felt disgust knowing she had not truly grieved, as her dependents were still clearly grieving, the death of her second husband. Rather, Jacqueline Laithe was emboldened by a vitality that had come at the same time of Benton's passing, and which had also brought an end to the only real grief she had ever known, the passing of Philmore. Indeed, her first marriage had been underpinned by love instead of greed or possession; but now, Jacqueline had sought another union (just as with Benton) that was rooted in her skewed conviction of maintaining her first husband's honor."

The reverend nodded. He was still working on something. "The flowers, Dean," he said with hollowed-out persistence. "What use had the flowers been given?"

"I looked toward the living room, at the fan on the ceiling that once held Benton's lifeless body, and saw a family of muted white blossoms hanging upside-down, tied to the supports with string. I could only assume these were the flowers that you mentioned were hanging elsewhere in the house. I also wanted there to be some greater significance to Jacqueline's preservation of them. However, after seeing their placement in that very spot, I saw their use for this final act of remembrance. Tell me, Reverend, what you see here— if not more than a simple memorial effort of a lamenting family?"

Milton uncrossed his fingers and scratched the stubble on his chin. He seemed preoccupied with this, as if he wished there was something else.

"Furthermore," I said, "if what you say of Jedediah's residency is true, and that therefore her proprietorship is limited despite his loss of sight and increased dependency— would it not relieve Jacqueline Laithe to see his current decline in health? She was the widow of the firstborn, after all—you've read the will. Why, she might even wish him to go all the way; for then she would be given full rights to it!" I finished, letting the connotation of my words settle on the dead air of the chamber as I looked into Milton's eyes.

He had nothing to contend.

Jacqueline

What kind of gall—what kind of *madness* did it require for someone to walk into the front door of our house, as she did on that day, and act as though she had always lived there? I made up my mind that I would put my plan into motion at first light. But who else could it have been to parade up the drive on that bleak-gray morning, walk in through the front door, put her bag down in the foyer, and start cleaning the house as if she had always lived there—who else than Ms. Rachel Graft in the flesh?

Not just any flesh either, but the sagging skin of old age with the bygones of yesterday's youth still clinging to her frail frame. Hatred burned in my heart toward this last obstacle preventing me from taking the land back; taking Philmore's land back, nonetheless, which had become Benton's, and finally belonged to Jed and I—one of whom was only barely hanging onto his own life.

Phil left the world a daughter, of course, but she had become acquainted with trauma, loss, and friendlessness; and these made her scarcely recognizable. The land was mine to take, but evidently my dream was to be diverted from its destiny that morning with the arrival of Jedediah's birth mother through the front door and into the estate as if she had always lived in it.

"Who are you?" I said, with no animosity or ulterior condescension, other than that poised protection one feels over her property.

"Your mother-in-law, dear," she said, plain as can be. "As I imagine I've recently become."

The fire, a burning torrent in my soul, licked with stronger flames as I realized the trick of fate: that the day I had decided to take back my husband's land was the same day that this last harrowing lieutenant of evil and unknown origin came striding into the house in defiance of me. Yet it was not enough to stop my ultimate plan, nor my malice-borne persistence in possessing the land. I told Rachel to make herself comfortable, and that no matter how long she needed to stay—I assured her—the Laithe estate welcomed her warmly.

"Take my old room," I said. "First door on the right, down the hall."

It was only dawn, and I decided to cede the battle to win the war. I felt excitement in my chest and an uneasy anticipation of any more threats to prevent themselves in that dewy hour of morning, when cold light harbored before daybreak and soon moored itself to the windowsills. I continued with my plan and turned back toward the stove.

They introduced themselves to each other timidly enough at first, mother and son, then Rachel drew near to the poor human whose sight had been robbed by his latent manifestations of grief in losing Benton. I myself had even cultivated and encouraged a kind of reverence for the name of my second husband. Even though Benton was not my true love, he had been a love nevertheless, and gave his life for the world to be purified of pain. That was how I saw it. His death was a surrender to the forces of evil which had put up a battlement of their own. And he had fortified himself with an unseeable resilience; unachievable except by those who have also been in war and seen artillery severing trees and human limbs with their very eyes. Therefore, despite my eagerness to put his memory to rest, I occasioned a remembrance of my own: setting a peck of bloodroot to the side and hanging them where the war-torn martyr was last seen hanging under the ceiling fan.

I had not known that war, but I had known a war just the same—the small degradation that happened in the human heart between consecutive losses within the same house, and the tightness within the walls of my chest that carried the grief of the first to bear the second. I loved Philmore and loved him well, I submitted to Benton and understood his soul, and now I had married the third in the line for the sole purpose of lessening his burden and putting his light out.

It was the culmination of the long war that I hoped for, the end to the struggle in my own life against Fate's many guises of suffering. These inroads were being trodden now in the deterioration of Jedediah's sight, but the way forward was less clear after the return of his birth mother to care for him as his end drew near. I knew she was not a blessing. Nor was she the good fortune that Jed thought she was.

I decided I would still carry out my duty that day; but there were many moments when I thought about giving it up—my whole plan—and taking the orange-red roots out of the ice box, throwing them in the creek, and submitting to the slow-marching foot soldiers of Time. The moment I most considered this alternative was later, when the reverend's wife showed up at the estate. For then I was outnumbered.

Deaconess Sarah

The only thing the Devil loved more than a man falling was the woman behind it. I knew, because I'd been married to a man who had never fallen in 43 years of marriage—and yes, love could last that long. It still amazed me, how I was ushered that long ago without my knowing, into the *only* life a minister's wife would ever know—sheltering the young women in the church who wielded the power to make great men fall.

I already stood upon the porch of the Laithe estate before I questioned whether I knew what I had gotten myself into. It was a cold-lit morning. There had been perhaps a dozen, *no that's not quite right,* half a dozen, deer along the road on my way through the woods surrounding Newburg. I even saw an albino deer—sleek white and poised in a field, likely scoping out new terrain for the long winter approaching. It was delightful to watch animals and the earth and the sky, but these images were all things I was using to tarry my entrance into the estate. *A shame,* I thought. *I'm stronger than that.*

I ascended the steps and knocked twice at the door, waiting patiently. The knock remained unanswered, but there was some sound of stirring within. I walked along the wraparound porch and saw a window ajar.

"Jackie!" I said. "It's me. Sarah."

I came back to the front and saw that the door had been unlocked and opened. It was only cracked, but wide enough to suggest I was welcome.

"Hiya, Jacqueline," I said, walking into the foyer. "I cooked you some pumpkin pie. Milton and I were wondering how you were getting along."

"Thank you, Sarah," Jacqueline said, taking the dish from me. "I imagine you're missing church this morning just for the errand. I would invite you to stay but it's been an unusually tough one."

The furrow in her brow flickered, lines in her forehead relaxed for a second as if she had been forcing a look of weariness and momentarily took a break. I had seen the game of emotional charades before—I was used to womanly defenses.

"What's wrong, honey?" I said.

She retreated back to the kitchen and, placing the dish on the stove top, carried on with the preparation of a meal. Jacqueline's hands were fretful, slight, and betrayed. I felt almost like I had intruded upon her in the act of something defiant and crude. This was not altogether new to me regarding women of her age, but there was something more. Something I couldn't gauge.

"What are you preparing there, Jacqueline?" I asked, keeping it light. She had out a bowl and a grinding tool that turned what looked like stalks into a baby-food mush. There was a tray of orange-red herbs beside the mixing bowl.

"Some food for my hungry *husband*," she said, making a smile that the light hit in a revealing way. I could tell she hadn't intended to give away anything by her expression. Her marriage *was* new to me, but I attempted not to react to the word she used in reference to Jed. This was always the right way with other women—take it at face value and digest it later. I looked over to where Jedediah sat at the table and said hello to him, seeing another figure silhouetted against the windows.

"Is that Sarah?" he said back.

"It is she," I said, "but I was just leaving, Jed." I saw his eyes then; it was as though they were filled with murky well water that reflected an unnaturally white hue. I saw he was afflicted, or had a condition.

"This's my mama, Sarah," he said. "Came a few days ago to give my wife a hand with things."

"It's a pleasure, Rachel—Rachel, isn't it?" I said.

She was surprised I knew of her, but I tried to prevent any feigned look of pleasure. Over the years, I had also seen what the absence of mothers had done to grown men later in life, like Jed. Milton and I had been around The Captain a lot, since the Laithe name held much weight in Newburg and he had been a man forever in danger of falling. I knew of Rachel but had always pretended she never existed, so I avoided betraying my own protectiveness of Jed or his family by giving her any undue attention.

My question was yet unanswered by Jacqueline, but she kept crushing her spices with the mortar and pestle. It felt strange—there was something Romanesque about it, to give it a word. I needed to hurry to the part where I digested this scene, so I said:

"We've missed you at church, Jackie. Let me know when you need an extra hand, okay? I better get along, but if you need a place to go for the holidays, I'm cooking two turkeys this year. Plenty for—"

Before I could finish, a fit of coughing rose from a back room—wheezing, droning on until Jackie looked at Rachel, who abandoned her seat beside Jed and hurried down the hall to the source. It left me alone with Jacqueline and Jedediah, who had his head leaned back now; he was listening for the noises, the soft cooing sound of his long-lost mother tending to Harmony. I had no idea of the girl's condition from whatever corner of the house she now inhabited, but it sounded as though she had been touched by a wicked disease. I determined I would pray for them, over them, among them, and that my devotion to winning the Laithe family over would be a dutiful one—as any strong wife ought to do on behalf of her husband's church. I decided to return home and call on Jacqueline the next day. As I left, I thought of the deer from earlier that morning; the family and the way the doe nurtured the young, and the all-white one with its head raised in indomitable awareness.

In the Scriptures, Delilah had had many nights to deal the ultimate blow to her husband. I feared Jacqueline was capable of something similar, for she also was a robust woman. But ultimately, I felt encouragement reflecting on what I had seen: the image of Jacqueline preparing her husband a meal, turning the orange-red roots to mush in the mortar for some medicinal use perhaps, and the soft shushing and cooing of Rachel tending to the young. It was just like the deer.

Harmony

Words stopped coming to me. I followed the trail of my thoughts—*it was no use when your skin felt like it was melting*. I wished to God I hadn't done it with her that night. Why had I done it? Every time I thought I was finding my way back to Addie in my head, she died all over again. If I had died instead it would've been almost better than the way it turned out. Nowadays I woke up in the night screaming.

Sometimes Jackie, sometimes Jedediah, would fumble into the room. Blind man...old dumb dying man Jed. Jackie came and put a hot rag—a wet, hot rag—right on my head. One morning some stranger did it. Swear to God I never met her in my life and there she was in my ear like I came from her womb.

"Shhh, Harmony, shhh. I'm Rachel. Jackie knows me...needs me to take care of you now while she feeds your uncle."

I couldn't say anything back even if I wanted to. Saying words was even harder than thinking them when you were getting off smack. *But who cared, anyway?* It wouldn't matter at the end of the day (if there was an end to a day) with my body feeling like it had sunburns all over and wrapped in a blanket.

There was a dying that had to be done. Just wondered which of us would go first—me or Jed. He had me in years but I had him in opioids. I'd started off so strong, too; the way I'd held him when he was wailing about Benton, not even letting my own agony rip me apart about Adelaide.

That's why I kept getting the powder across the river. Might as well make the old rounds even if I'd be in bed for weeks after I quit, feeling the whole-body fire of withdrawals and getting used to strangers shushing in my ear like they knew me. I guess we were family now, though, this Rachel and I.

I couldn't even remember things like they were. Words wouldn't come, melodies from songs didn't click. There was the one Addie taught me, but what was the use in that. *Right*? What was the use. Addie must've known something I didn't. Died right there with the song, right there with Uncle Ben.

Words wouldn't come, days were longer than gone. For Jedediah and me, suffering had begun without the memories or melodies to make it bearable. What was grief, trauma, life, death and enduring? If I died from this, Jed would be right behind me. If I endured, would life be worth the living, or was dying a kind of renewing too? Better yet, I kept wondering: *Is there a pasture for the soul as green as springtime; a place to go after life?*

Jedediah

Sight or no sight, it was just about the same when you lived off the lan' around a village like Newburg, a cyst of a town where kids ran barefoot into brambles and briers and couldn't even hear their parents calling them back for supper. What was the use of the eyes we were given—to assume we knew more about the world just because it came to us in shapes and colors? Nowadays, shapes were only what I could feel with my fingers; and all of a sudden, I could only see by hearin'. Could only watch the world with taste and touch.

I was a young boy once and Miss'ura was my mother at birth. But now she was joined by my mother at death—my other mother who came back to me after I called to her from the window with the wallpaper curling down when Benton was clamorin' out back against the whisperin' trees that August day. I reckoned I didn't have much longer, but Rachel came 'fore I kicked it at least. I didn't know how much time I had left.

It was that scrapin'-on after life, the hollowed clash against the crucible I still heard, and myself bein' on the verge of knowin' what it was like in the great darkness yonder. I would take my wife just as she was though—my wife I had never deserved and even less should be worth havin' than the ol' boy who couldn't shake the war and so shook the burden off himself to go toward his own darkness.

Benton and the glass and that spect'cle made sense to me now. Figured I knew why he was always at that range. The temperin' and the holdin'-onto that the furnace was good for—it was like the hollowin' out o' the earth beneath the pickaxe, or the way we tunneled through the flesh of our mamas and came out into the world on the other side of glory; on the here-side of misery, in Miss'ura, on this gospel ground which nurtured us and coddled us when we were babies.

I could smell stew on the stove in the kitchen and heard the flies in there buzzin', listening to Jackie cut up the food from the garden and thinkin' how she was my own love before I knew I could have one. She was my love even when my jealous pride and anger weren't takin' care o' her like she ought'a be. I'd always wanted her; I knew now. Maybe it was wrong to want her all that time, seein' she was my brothers' before she was mine, but it only made her more o' my flesh and my blood. It wasn't real blood, so I reckoned I wasn't doin' so great a sin as The Cap'n had done. Still, they were all here: my blood and my almost-blood. My head was drawn near Rachel's chest and I wanted to bury my head in her breasts on the rocking chair again like I had when I was younger.

But the season had passed, the cows had come home, someone had taken my crop and my field and the life I once lived; I couldn't see the world. I could only hear it. I asked Dean to take care o' the estate, so he got us a new lawyer. I wanted my mother; now she was mine. I had always wanted Jackie; and now she would love me, and I would love her like I always had. *This was the way a Miss'ura man ought to die*, I thought.

Just then someone came in, and I knew it was the ol' reverend's wife once she spoke to Jackie. It made me proud and almost shy of my pride to introduce the deaconess to my mama. Sarah seemed to know of Rachel, but didn't trust her yet. Maybe she would in time, though.

My life was gettin' better for the first time since the day Benton left me with nothin' but a memory and a whisper of his pain. He was grit, that boy, and I was the man o' the family now. I was even carrying on for Phil, makin' good on my vow to look after his lady and his daughter—that girl who was not present in the room but soon started coughin' and makin' a fit in the back of the house.

The soft fabric against my cheek went away— Mama's blouse and breasts gone—and I was still there in the blackness smellin' the stew and hearing it boil. Harmony was having a tantrum that could'a called the hellhounds in and still not ceased. I reckoned it was okay that Rachel should check on her. I leaned my head back, listenin' to that soft:

"There, there, Harmony," Rachel said, delicate, like Harmony had gone back in time to infancy again or even back to the darkness o' the womb. "How's that, baby? Take my hand. Put this blanket here, you see? Good. Prop your head up, honey."

Finally, the reverend's wife left so the Laithe family could carry on as it should. A little time passed and I heard the cooin' die down. Mama still wasn't with me, but steam rose to my face and made my skin and nostrils open up. The smell of the stew came strong, served in a bowl and put before me by my wife who sat with me at the table now.

She knew I was hurtin'. She could tell losin' the Sight was too much for a man who worked with his hands. I could hear her say, "Just a few spoonfuls, Jed. Like this— there." And the soup running down my chin but the taste comin' to me fast like an old summer years ago. "Thank you, Jackie," I said. "You are my own."

I was still workin' up to the *love* word, but my chest felt tight, my throat got smaller, almost as it had that day I tried checkin' on Jackie and it got all chalky. It didn't feel right, like I almost couldn't breathe. Like I—

Reverend Milton

The hard-earth smell was everywhere. A yellow odor in the church rose and pressed up beneath the musty air that came down from the steeple. The bells had ceased ringing, drawing the people of Newburg in and ushering the Spirit with them. The trees outside stood naked, their shivering boughs bare like a newborn child. There was cold light, hard and brittle, coming into the sanctuary through the stained glass. It partially illuminated the baptistery, and the light crawled down the steps to the back of the church where I left my chamber to approach the lectern. Before ascending the stage during the last hymn, I looked out through the window that looked over the valley. The land was stretched over the hills, the ground rolled out from beneath itself to find the rivers and streams and the lowland.

It was unspoken, the beauty that endured when you couldn't see the end of the sky. It seemed as if it would go on forever, on and on; if you could only make the next hill, you might see the end of it. *A place to grow old and die.* It was. My wife called it "open-sky country."

Sarah didn't need anything but the rolling hills and her faith. And what a blessing that was—not to worry about a woman's pleasure but to be wholly concerned with the Lord's. To be content in it and never stray from it. My ministry wouldn't be possible without her, in fact; for when there were too many sheep to keep track of, I'd have to send her off to find the stray ones for me. That was how it was that November morning.

Sarah offered to miss the first service so she could check on Jacqueline and her family. The rumors were that Jacqueline was overwhelmed with her husband's health condition, and her daughter's rehabilitation had put a heavy strain on her. It was hard for any woman taking on a load like that, but I also had my suspicions that Jacqueline was no ordinary woman. She might've even been called favored, the way it seemed the Lord kept watching out for her in all the legal matters she could possibly see to. There were few truly good women, and even fewer good men in those days; and the women that were good were the only worthwhile pursuit of any man. It was tricky business, this finding of a partner to further one's ministry—I must have been favored also, since it happened to me. But thankfully, God made it easier by giving us a way of discerning good women. That was my message that morning. I heard the hymn die out, and the suspension of voices in the air cease, before I pulled back the curtain and walked up the side steps toward the lectern.

"The Judges 5 woman, Jael, is the woman who should be most feared; for she does not wait for others to do her bidding. She sees and is committed to action. See, in verses 24-26, how the Lord praises this woman, for she has conquered a great warrior in his sleep.

Blessed above women shall Jael the wife of
Heber the Kenite be,
Blessed shall she be above women in the tent.
He asked for water, and she gave him milk;
She brought forth butter in a lordly dish.
She put her hand to the nail,
And her right hand to the workmen's
hammer;
And with the hammer she smote Sisera, she
smote off his head,
When she had pierced and stricken through
his temples.

"You were taught that the only woman a man should find, and serve, and love as the Scriptures command, is the Proverbs 31 woman. It is not so. I tell the congregation this morning, humble yourself to accept that there is power in a woman of God committed to action. And who was Sisera, that he was smote in so lowly a manner? The lesson here: that a great warrior does not sleep in the presence of his enemies—and that he does not underestimate the woman. Let us see now, how the seeds of lament are sown in those the warrior has left behind."

The mother of Sisera looked out at a
window, and cried through the lattice,

Why is his chariot so long in coming? Why tarry the wheels of his chariots?

"Of all those in the story, the mother of Sisera is most to be pitied. Yet this verse is not about her loss, but rather Jael's gain and cunning at a time when her enemy was defenseless. May we all keep watch, and favor the woman who answers the door when opportunity knocks."

I presented God's message with sincerity. The rest of the sermon was delivered with that same diligence; and after the service, the phone began ringing in my chambers. I answered it.

"Milton?" a voice said. It wasn't my wife's, who I was expecting, but Jacqueline's.

"Is it Jed?" I said.

"Yes. He's just fallen awfully sick."

"Tell my wife to stay there," I said.

"She left a while ago, Reverend." Jacqueline said. Her voice was quivering, but something about it was false. "Come Milton, please," she said. "The paramedics are with him now...he was asking for you."

Jedediah had always said Benton looked like a dog when he died, covered up by the family rug; but Jedediah himself looked like a dying hound underneath the covers of the bed in that old room he'd once slept in long ago—with the edges of the wallpaper curling at the corners. He didn't have much longer when I arrived. I simply put my hand on his chest and heard the air barely making it through his throat, constricted.

The first responders had cleared the furniture, and the room was bare except for a bed and a stranger trapped in the frail frame of Jedediah Laithe. It was evidently too dangerous to move him to a hospital yet. I prayed over him and felt his chest rise and fall in slight compressions that only suggested life rather than proving it. Soon there were none at all, and I had to move away from the commotion.

The house took on a different medium, a semidarkness between the nocturnal shades of night and the harking brightness of dawn. The last of the Laithe men leveled; the circle complete, but the unwinding only just having begun in the society of Newburg. You could feel it. The ethereal madness took root in the stone foundations of the estate. And walking out, I met the thrice-widowed woman on the porch.

"My condolences, Jackie," I said, watching her face for a sign that her grief could be real; that the marriage was not just a hoax, and I not merely the fool in blessing it. "Your husband is at peace now."

"Thank you, Reverend," Jacqueline said.

The corner of her mouth bent upward almost unnoticeably. It was unsettling in a prophetic way, like the adulteress in Proverbs whose feet led down to Sheol, but who disguised her deceit with a veil of modesty. I felt ashamed of immediately associating an image of immorality with the bereaved, so I dismissed myself from her and began my walk down the hallowed, dark, descending drive. I was walking by the old garden, the lifeless ground now, that still showed shriveled roots and colorless petals within the folds of hardened earth. It was a voice from the house, however, that stopped me.

"Milton!" a woman said through a window in the front of the house. "Will his soul be in heaven?"

I recognized who it was immediately. Jedediah's mother, back from a lifetime of silence; still, I did not weaponize my faith against her.

"If God is faithful to him—and I believe he is to all of us in our time—he will be saved," I said, drawing nearer now so she could hear me. I could see her face through the pane, a look of real grief despite her absence during nearly all of her son's life. Rachel let out a heavy breath and looked past me down the drive, where a car turned in the lane. She spoke with the marbled sound of longing in her voice.

"I think I hear a car, Reverend! Tell me, is that the coroner coming up the hill?"

THE END

Acknowledgements

To Meghan Jenkins for telling me I had a voice; if not for that nudge, I'm not sure this ever would have been written.

To Seth McKinney; for showing me what didn't work, and pushing me to find what did.

To Evan Söell, a friend closer than family, and John Wissmiller, my anchor; for sharing your dreams with me.

To Katelyn Johnson, writer and mentor; who babysat my poetry before it could graduate to prose.

To Naomi Nero, whose fingerprints were all over *Chariot* from plot screening to print; it could not have been done without you.

To Charlie Ferebee, my editor, for asking the most of me; your grasp of style and love of the craft won the day.

To Madison Wisse, my illustrator; for giving this work dignity with your art. There was not a moment you missed my vision.

To Josh Frank, who helped me get in this business. Thank you.

To my family:

>Mom and Dad, for being a sound in the river; a safe place to grow my roots.

>Logan, my first reader and constant supporter of my creative efforts.

>Austin, whose love of literature kindled mine.

>Tesni, learning to talk, and Acadia finding her firsts also.

>Maime, whose life is her family; whose love was my Papa.

>This is all for you.

Note From Author

There is not enough time to thank the people whose contributions were small but equally as valuable to me. Of course I can try, but it will not be enough. Thomas Massion, you handed me Stephen King's Memoir On Writing circa June 2021 and it made me realize what was possible. That was a good step. We held conversations, and those were what shed the impossibility. Both were needed for me to get here. Emin Fatih Özdem—Emfa. No one shows affection like a Turkish brother. There is a room in my heart for you, and you are welcome there. Dr. Mary Reidmeyer, I saw your eyes glow next to the crucible when you showed me what it means to you. I pray I did your craft justice.

I think on the way that writing is like bailing out water. If life can be dramatized to the sinking ship, the excess water is taken out too slow to reverse it; yet writing is still the pail which has kept me afloat in dark times, and for that I am humbled. I am undeserving of this gift, and furthermore, am without a way to say thank you enough to you—the one who supported me and read this story, and met me on the stern with a bucket. You are indispensable. Godspeed and good tidings from your author.

Made in the USA
Las Vegas, NV
15 November 2022